"That's all you remember? Just your name?"

"And my age." *Tell her you're a Ranger,* the honorable side of him scolded the other part that foolishly refused to confess. It felt as if everything would slam back into place once tomorrow dawned, so would it be terrible to just keep this one night as the happy victory it was?

"For a while there I was terrified it wouldn't come back. That I'd end up one of those freak stories you read about in checkout counter tabloids."

She laughed. "I can't imagine you up there with the celebrity tragedies and alien babies. You're far too normal."

Normal? Nothing about him felt normal. The scary part was the constant sense that his normal wasn't anywhere near as nice as right now was, sitting out under the stars near a roaring fire hearing Christmas carols.

Finn waited for his unnamed aversion to all things Christmas to wash up over him. Why couldn't he grasp the big dark thing lurking just out of his reach?

* * *

Lone Star Cowboy League:
Bighearted ranchers in small-town Texas

Allie Pleiter, an award-winning author and RITA®
Award finalist, writes both fiction and nonfiction. Her
passion for knitting shows up in many of her books
and all over her life. Entirely too fond of French
macarons and lemon meringue pie, Allie spends her
days writing books and avoiding housework. Allie
grew up in Connecticut, holds a BS in speech from
Northwestern University and lives near Chicago,
Illinois.

A Ranger
for the Holidays

Allie Pleiter

HHARLEQUIN® LOVE INSPIRED®

Special thanks and acknowledgment to Allie Pleiter
for her contribution to the Lone Star Cowboy League miniseries.

Recycling programs
for this product may
not exist in your area.

™ LOVE INSPIRED BOOKS

ISBN-13: 978-0-373-81876-1

A Ranger for the Holidays

Copyright © 2015 by Harlequin Books S.A.

www.Harlequin.com

Printed in U.S.A.

Forget the former things;
do not dwell on the past.
See, I am doing a new thing!
Now it springs up; do you not perceive it?
I am making a way in the wilderness
and streams in the wasteland.
—*Isaiah* 43:18–19

To Barb
Welcome to the family

Chapter One

Pine trees don't wear gloves.

Amelia Klondike, like any sensible person on God's earth, knew that. She was out here in the woods to find pinecones for a Sunday school project, not accessories. She set down the last of the lemon bar and coffee she'd brought for breakfast—Amelia didn't believe in sensible breakfasts, ever—and picked up the glove from its place among the scattered pinecones. Large, well made, worn to a comfortable softness, it was definitely a man's glove—one that would be missed, so she should try to find its owner. She chuckled as her mind made the connection; a woman whose life's work was a charity called Here to Help ought to be able to help one glove find the man who owned it.

Not that Amelia was looking to find a man—gloved or otherwise—these days. Just over a year out from a publicly broken engagement, Amelia was barely starting to feel as if talk had died down and she could be seen as Little Horn's best helping hand, not its saddest broken heart.

She was tucking the glove in her pocket when she spotted its mate ten feet away. Then a boot… and a leg…until there, lying under the largest of the pine trees, Amelia spied the owner of those gloves.

She blinked a few times, startled to see a large, ruggedly dressed man sprawled in the wet needles under the boughs. "Sir?" The angle of his arms and legs wasn't that of sleep, and last night's storm certainly wasn't conducive to camping out under the stars. Amelia dropped the gloves and her pack on the ground and walked over to shake the man's shoulder. "Hey, sir, are you all right?"

He didn't respond. *Lord, help me, what do I do?* she prayed as she looked around for any sign of companions or transportation. Short of Louie, her own horse, who stood inspecting a clump of grass behind her, Amelia was alone. She didn't recognize the rather handsome man; he was clean-cut, well if casually dressed, but mud-smeared as if he'd been out here all night. As if he'd come to some kind of mishap. "Are you hurt? Sick? You don't look like you should…"

Amelia swallowed her words as the man groaned and turned his head to reveal a grisly wound across his forehead. "Oh, mercy!" Amelia gasped, fumbling back to her backpack for her cell phone. She had to call 911. This man needed an ambulance.

The phone was no help—she should have known she'd get no cell service way out here. How was she going to get this poor soul to help? Amelia twisted a blond curl around her fingers in panicked consideration of her options. Sometimes text got through on almost no service and she was good friends with Lucy Benson, the sheriff. Would Lucy be nearby on a Saturday morning? She pulled up Lucy's cell number and typed Emergency!

She shook the man gently, pulling the scarf from her neck to wipe the worst of the drying blood from his face. Someone—or something—had taken a good whack at his forehead. Accident? Fight? Bandit? Little Horn had been experiencing its own odd crime spree in recent weeks, so there was no telling if the attractive man on the ground before her was a good guy or a bad one. If the past year had taught her anything, it was that bad guys could come in good-looking packages.

Hero or villain, this was a hurt man in need of help, and right now she was the only help to be had. Carefully, she rolled him fully onto his back, which made him wince. "Sorry about this," she offered as she rummaged through his pockets for a phone, wallet or, hopefully, car keys to a truck just out of sight.

The search came up empty. No keys, no wallet, no phone. "Looks like someone had it in for you, mister." Given all the robberies taking place in Little Horn of late, it wasn't hard to think the criminals had expanded their cattle and equipment theft to face-to-face holdups. It took a special brand of mean to not only take a man's valuables, but to dump him unconscious in the middle of nowhere. "Come on there, cowboy, wake up. This'd be a whole lot easier with you conscious."

Her phone dinged an incoming text from Lucy. Hurt? Gramps?

It would be natural for Lucy to think any emergency of Amelia's involved the elderly grandfather who lived with her, but not this time. Found injured man in woods just over ridge behind Palmer's Creek. Call 9-1-1 for me?

I'm not too far from there. On my way.

Some days it paid well to be best friends with the local sheriff. "Help is on the way," she told the unconscious man. Wasn't it important to keep concussion victims awake? Why hadn't she paid more attention when watching medical dramas?

Try talking to him. She grasped one of his broad, solid shoulders and shook him a little harder. "Do you hurt anywhere? What's your name?"

No response other than a groan, but he had moved his hand and Amelia spied a watch. "Why'd they leave your watch when they took everything else?" She began unbuckling the old, worn timepiece—it was a long shot, but maybe the watch could at least give her a name or initials if it was engraved.

It was. *Finn: all my love, B.* Mystery man had a name—and someone who missed him. "You're no slouch to look at, Finn, B's a lucky lady. And worried, I expect." She'd spent enough time praying for her now-ex-fiancé, Rafe, to come off duty from the Texas Rangers safe and sound that her heart twisted in sympathy for the likely frantic B. It looked as if Finn had been out here all night, if not longer. "Wake up, Finn." She leaned in closer to his fine features. "Finn! Finn, can you hear me?"

A hint of awareness washed over the man's features. He dwarfed her—she guessed him to be over six feet tall and very fit. "Can you sit up?" She tried to pull his chest vertical, but he winced and his eyes shot wide open. They locked on to her for a second, a startling sky blue contrast to his glossy dark brown hair, before losing focus again as he fell back to the ground and murmured, "Ouch."

"I guess you're more hurt than you look." Amelia pushed up the fleece he wore to see blood staining the shirt underneath. "Mercy, Finn, I don't think you should move at all. Help is on the way, so you just sit still."

His hand moved to his chest. "Ribs." He said, the word slurring a bit.

"You might have cracked a few of those, and you're definitely bleeding." She took her scarf from behind his head and bunched it up against the red spot on his shirt. "Stay with me, Finn. Keep those eyes open." She grabbed Finn's hand, finding it alarmingly cold, and guided it to press against the scarf on his wound. His eyes found her again, the fear and confusion in his gaze going straight to the pit of her stomach.

"My name's Amelia, and I'm getting you help." She bit her lip. "You just stick with me, okay?"

Finn nodded his head. When he coughed, she could see the pain shoot through him even as he grabbed her hand. "Where am...?" Finn's words fell off into a sharp hiss as he tried to rise again.

Amelia put a hand gently to his shoulder. "Oh, no, you don't. You'd better stay still."

Finn's eyes wandered again, then returned to her as he let his head fall back against the ground.

He looked at her as if she was the only person in his world—and right now, wasn't she? "Where am I?" he asked in halting words.

"You're in…well, the middle of nowhere, really." She grabbed his free hand—the one where the watch had been—and held it, stroking his forearm in an effort to keep him calm. *Keep him talking to you.* "What on earth made you come up into the forest in last night's storm? Or did someone just dump you here?"

"I…" Finn's eyes rolled back and his lids fell shut. The hand Amelia was touching lost its tension and dropped to his chest.

He'd lost consciousness again—that couldn't be good news. "Lord," Amelia prayed aloud, helplessness pushing her pulse higher, "I need to know what to do here. Don't You let Finn die before help comes. Don't You do that to him or to me." She laid her hand against Finn's chest, grateful to feel breath and a heartbeat.

Amelia checked her phone again, then used the edge of her jacket to blot the sheen of sweat now beading Finn's forehead. "Finn? Finn, wake up. Show me those nice blue eyes." She grabbed his hand again, shaking it a bit to rouse him. "I found your gloves." That struck her as a ridiculous thing to say, but she didn't have a lot of experience making conversation with men out cold. Gramps fell asleep nightly—okay, hourly—in his recliner, but that was different. "Come on, Finn, give a gal a break. Open your eyes. Groan a little. Let me know you're still in there."

Finn seemed to grow more still, even the tension in his rugged features going soft as if falling sleep. Was he dying? He was such a nice-looking guy—if she discounted the mud, leaves and blood. Far too dashing to meet his end out here in a pile of pine needles.

Her phone beeped again. Shout out the text from Lucy said. Amelia dropped Finn's hand and stood to yell "Lucy!" at the top of her lungs. She heard the distant rumble of an engine and dashed over to the side of the ridge to see a little all-terrain vehicle scrambling up the hillside with Lucy's white police SUV not far behind. Some distance back, Amelia could see the flashing lights of what had to be an ambulance.

"Here!" Amelia yelled again, jumping up and down and waving her arms as relief filled her chest. "Over here!"

When the ATV veered in her direction, Amelia dashed back to Finn, still motionless on the ground.

"It's okay, Finn," she said, mopping his face again. "We're gonna get you out of here." She grabbed his hand, breathless and surprisingly near tears. "Help is here. You're safe."

* * *

"Hello there. Welcome back. I'm Dr. Searle." A man in tortoiseshell glasses was peering at him as if he was a science experiment. The doctor's warm tone felt suspiciously rehearsed. "Can you tell me your name?"

His name? His name seemed just out of reach. The combination of pain and confusion left him feeling weightless and heavy at the same time— as if he couldn't tell up from down or left from right. He couldn't answer.

The doctor adjusted his glasses. "Amelia found a watch on your wrist inscribed to Finn. Is that your name?"

"Sounds…right," he said, mostly because he didn't know what else to say. Amelia? Did he know that name?

"Well, let's go with Finn for now. Tell me, can you see my face clearly?" Dr. Searle asked.

"Uh…I guess so." Glory, even his teeth hurt. His tongue felt dry and sluggish. Where did this awful headache come from? Why did everything feel so out of place?

Dr. Searle switched on a small light and waved it back and forth. "Do you know where you are?"

"No." Admitting that made the pounding in his head go double-time, a steady rhythm of *not-good, not-good, not-good*.

"You're in the Little Horn Regional Medical

Center. Amelia Klondike found you unconscious in the woods early this morning. Can you tell me how you got there?"

The pounding turned into a slam, with a sucker punch of fear to his gut. "No." Hospital? In the woods? Out cold? Come to think of it, he couldn't remember anything about *anything* except that this Amelia person sounded a bit familiar. The air turned thin and his head began to spin. "My head hurts. And my ribs."

"I expect so. You've had a concussion, along with a few broken ribs and several nasty lacerations. Whatever hit you was big and mean. Took your wallet and your phone and left you out in the storm from the looks of it. Amelia said you had nothing on you but the watch."

Amelia. He focused on the half-familiar name and remembered a vague impression of some very pretty blue eyes and a soft, soothing voice. Everything else was a blank.

"Well, Finn, it seems the knock on your head has rattled things around a bit. I'd try not to worry about it. It's not that unusual for head-trauma patients to lose the hours around their injury at first."

Finn didn't like that he'd said "that unusual." And he hadn't just lost a few hours—right now it felt as if he'd lost everything. The spinning started again and he closed his eyes.

"I'm going to run some tests and give your

description to the police. We might not be able to learn much over the weekend, but it's worth a shot. Can you tell me if Finn is your first name, a last name or a nickname?"

Finn licked his dry, cracked lips. It hurt to think. For that matter, it hurt to breathe. "I don't know." He put his hand to his forehead, immediately regretting the sparks of pain it sent through the back of his eyes.

The doctor put a hand on Finn's arm. "Try not to get all worked up. You must have friends or family looking for you. It won't take long to sort things out."

If Dr. Searle could have picked the one idea to make Finn feel worse… The haunting sense that no one was missing him or searching for him, that he was alone, was as deep as it was inexplicable. "I don't remember anything, Doc." It felt as if the admission swallowed him whole.

"It'll likely come back to you in the next few hours. Are you up for a visitor? Amelia's been out in the lobby waiting for you to wake up, and if you ask me, you could do with a distraction right about now."

"Sure." After all, this Amelia was the only thing he thought he remembered right now.

Dr. Searle gave him a half casual, half concerned smile as he moved to the door and opened it.

"Well, look at you, awake and everything."

"Amelia" swept into the room with a bouquet of flowers and a bundle of plaid fabric. The particular turquoise of her eyes did feel vaguely familiar, as did her voice. In fact, her voice and eyes were the only memory he could pull up at all.

She deposited the flowers on his bedside table with a hopeful smile. As rescue squads went, she was pretty easy on the eyes with a tumble of blond hair and a petite, curvy figure. "Do you remember me? I found you early this morning."

"A bit." He had no idea what to say.

"Dr. Searle says you'll recover just fine despite being pretty banged up. Gramps broke a rib once—I know it isn't much fun."

Should he know who Gramps was? "It's not." Finn stared at her, feeling as if he ought to know more about her but coming up short. All he remembered was the sound of her voice saying *You're safe* and the blue of her eyes. And her hand. He remembered her holding his hand. He started to say *You're the only thing I remember*, but changed his mind.

She mistook his silence for curiosity about the bundle, so she held up what turned out to be pajamas. "I think hospital gowns make you feel sicker than you already are. I figured you'd want to be comfortable, seeing as Doc Searle says you'll be here over the weekend while they run a bunch of tests. You look to me like a blue plaid kind of guy." She handed them to him, and when her fingers brushed his arm, the familiarity returned again. Something—anything familiar—made Finn fight the urge to grab her hand and hold it to see if the sensation would grow stronger.

Her face softened with concern. "So you don't remember anything?"

"I remember your voice saying I'd be okay."

That was the wrong thing to say—a flush pinked her cheeks and she looked away for an awkward moment. Finn felt foolish, lost and stumbling through this absurd situation.

"I've never met anyone with real, true amnesia before. I thought it only happened on soap operas."

Amnesia. The word made him cringe. He looked down at the pajamas rather than at her eyes, feeling more exposed than any hospital gown could achieve.

"You'll be all right, you know. Little Horn is a nice town, filled with nice people who'll lend a hand to anyone in a tight spot." She was talking to fill the awkward silence, clearly trying to put him at ease. "You do know you're in Texas, don't you?"

Finn was grateful to have one question he could answer. "The accents made that easy to figure out, yes." Amelia had that lilting, musical quality to her voice that made Texan women so easy to talk to. The sound of home…wherever in Texas that was for him. How could he not know something so simple as his name and address?

As if she heard his thoughts, Amelia said, "Well, you have to be from somewhere around here, too, given yours."

"I suppose."

"And you know it's just after Thanksgiving?" She looked optimistic and hopeful, as if it would be a victory for both of them if he said yes.

Finn pointed to the "Happy Thanksgiving" decoration still up on his room wall. "I hope I ate well." The near-joke surprised him. Her presence was the only thing that even came close to putting him at ease. Finn was thankful for her brightness against the black void he could feel lurking where his memory ought to have been.

"I'm sure this will all work itself out. Doc says your memory is likely to come back in bits and pieces over the next few days. I'll do my best to make sure you're comfortable while that happens and find your folks so they're not out of their minds with worry. You just focus on resting and getting better."

He really was injured, wasn't he? The more he thought about it, the more he hurt. It felt as if someone had drained his body like a bathtub— Finn felt empty and fragile. At a loss physically, mentally and even emotionally. He put his hands up to cover his face for a moment, worried he couldn't hold all the emptiness in. He didn't even know where to go once they let him out of here.

A hand touched his elbow—the familiar touch he so desperately needed. "Hey, hey there," she said softly. "I know this has got to be hard but, Finn, you're gonna be fine. We'll all help you until you know what's next, okay?"

"Thank you for helping me." It came out with more emotion than he would have liked.

"Well, that's me. I'm a professional helper." The cheery smile lit up her face again. "But I have to say, you're my first honest-to-goodness rescue."

She seemed so proud of it. It made him feel just a little bit less freakish. She tugged on a curl in her hair and he remembered—he *remembered*—her doing that. The whole world before her was a complete blank, but at least he could remember small details about her. "No kidding," he said, smiling himself.

They stared at each other for a moment, oddly connected and yet in reality complete strangers.

"Well," she said, breaking the quiet, "I've got to run some errands for the Lone Star League—that's our local community organization—and you've got some tests and paperwork to do, so how about I come back after supper to see how you're holding up?" She stood up. "I don't live very far away, so it's no trouble." She pointed at him, her brows furrowing in mock-seriousness. "I expect my rescue-ees to make a full recovery, so you've got your work cut out for you."

Finally, someone who didn't look at him as if he'd been damaged beyond repair. "Got it."

"See you later, Finn." Hearing her say it, his name did sound right. It wasn't much, but it was a start.

Chapter Two

Amelia caught Dr. Tyler Grainger, the local pediatrician, in the hallway when she came back to the Medical Center a few hours later.

"I heard about your dramatic rescue," Tyler said. "That's got to be a first for Here to Help, isn't it?"

"No one's more surprised than I," Amelia offered. "And speaking of surprises, word is you have one yourself."

She could see Tyler hesitate. After such a public split from her own fiancé, it wasn't hard to see why he might hold back his news. "So you heard I proposed to Eva?"

She made sure to give him a warm smile. "Good news travels almost as fast as gossip in Little Horn. Congratulations." She really was happy for the good doctor, and Eva was becoming a close friend, but the news still stung. Their engagement came on the heels of that of League president Carson Thorn and another of Amelia's friends Ruby Donnovan. Even Amelia's sister, Lizzie, was recently engaged—Little Horn was having as much of a wedding boom as a crime spree lately. "Well, I'd best get in to visit my new project."

Tyler looked at the package from Maggie's, the local coffee shop, in Amelia's hand. "The nurse told me you left some flowers in Ben Stillwater's room, too. That's a nice thing to do." Ben Stillwater was a young man from Little Horn currently in a coma from a riding accident. "Does this man know how fortunate he is to be a project of yours?" the doctor teased.

"If he doesn't, he will soon." Amelia waved as she pushed the hospital room door open.

Finn looked better. Her heart still twisted at the lost look in his eyes, the way he searched places and faces as if desperate for any anchor. He looked at her as if hers was the only face that held any meaning for him. The half-eaten dinner beside him stirred her sympathy. *Hospital food? If anyone needs the comfort of home cooking, it's someone who can't remember where home is.*

He noticed her looking at the plate. "I remembered I don't like peas." The comment brought the faintest hint of a smile to his features. Finn's mussed, lost-puppy charm kicked Amelia's compulsion to help up a notch. That helpfulness was her special gift, but it occasionally proved her greatest weakness.

"I don't care for myself, actually. My favorite food is pie. I'm extra partial to blueberry, but really, any pie will do."

She'd hoped he'd say something like *My favorite is apple*, but he only shrugged and said, "Who doesn't like pie?"

Amelia sat down, putting the bakery box on his bedside table. "I'm glad to hear you say that. I went for the basics—apple, cherry and, given the season, pumpkin."

He narrowed his eyes at her, startled. "You brought me pie?"

What kind of life had he led that a simple kindness seemed so foreign to him? "I am of the opinion that pie makes most things better," she explained as she retrieved a second box with her own slice of blueberry. "Actually," she added, fishing two plastic forks out of the bag, "I haven't met the situation that can't be improved by a good slice of pie." Amelia dismissed his bed tray to the other side of the room and replaced it with the selection of pie slices. "Anything look especially appealing?"

She watched as his startled expression warmed to a small smile. Small, a tiny bit forced, but enough to restore the striking quality of those light blue eyes. Against the white of his bandages and the brown-black gloss of his hair, his eyes drew her gaze, making her stare even though she knew better.

Picking up the fork, he scanned the selection. "I *think* I like pumpkin."

"Only one way to find out," Amelia cued as she picked up her own fork and dug in. Delicious. She hoped Finn thought so, too.

She watched in satisfaction as his face registered the gastronomic pleasure that was Maggie's Coffee Shop pies. "Oh—" he sighed in just the way she'd hoped he would "—that's good. Beats peas and whatever meat that was supposed to be." He took another bite. "Thank you kindly."

It was gratifying to see him even a little bit happy. "My pleasure."

After a third bite, he paused to look at her, his head cocked sideways in analysis. "If you don't mind my asking, why are you being so nice to a complete stranger?" The sad edge he gave those last two words poked Amelia under the ribs.

Amelia had trouble explaining her compulsion to help folks in need to good friends, much less to strangers like Finn. Only he wasn't a stranger. He was someone she was supposed to help. Someone she didn't find by accident, but by Providence. She recognized the pull toward his circumstances, the slow burn of burden in her heart that she'd come to know as her unique gift in God's kingdom. While life had taken away important people—her parents, her grandmother, Rafe— life had given her lots of funds and a generous heart. "I make it a practice to be nice to everybody. And you're not really a stranger anymore."

He didn't reply. Instead, he concentrated on a fourth bite of pie until his curiosity evidently got the better of him and he asked, "You're really nice to *everybody*?"

"Well—" she dug her fork into the luscious pie again, feeling her face flush that he'd called her on such an exaggeration "—I admit it's harder with some folks than others, but yes, I try to be." It was doubly hard with folks like Byron McKay. Byron, the vice president of the Lone Star Cowboy League and so mean that everyone hoped President Carson Thorn never had to step aside, had laid into her but good this afternoon about some silly detail of League business. "Truth is, today I needed this pie as much as you."

He sat back and looked at her a few heartbeats longer than he ought to have. "I can't imagine anyone giving you a hard time."

Amelia squeaked out a laugh, unsettled by his stare. "Oh, you'd be surprised." She felt the words tumble out of her, rushing against the rise of warmth under the blue scarf she wore. She remembered wiping his face with the white one she'd worn this morning—now stained beyond repair. "Little Horn may be small by big-city standards—" she felt her words speeding up, filling the too-warm space between them "—but there's no shortage of opinions and ornery personalities here. We've had tensions. We've got grumps and gossips. It's been a rough patch these past two months. Try the apple."

Finn did as requested, nodding his approval. "Tell me about Little Horn," he asked, then evidently seeing the surprise on her face, added, "Maybe some little detail will spark a memory, and right now your voice is the only one that feels familiar."

Amelia sat back in her chair. Finn's admission that he found her voice comforting rose an insistent little hum in her stomach. "Little Horn's the same as a hundred other small Texas towns, I guess," she started. He must be feeling the worst kind of lonely, to draw such a complete blank on his home and family and everything the way he had. She wanted to fill in as many details for him as she could, to take at least some of the shadows from the corners of his eyes. "Most folks are ranchers or the like, but—" and here she hoisted her slice of pie "—we've got some good cooks, a warm, welcoming church—and of course, very nice doctors. The sheriff, my friend Lucy? She says Little Horn is about as upright a place as can be—that is up until all the rustling that's been going on. That has everyone on edge."

"Cattle rustling?" His interest seemed to pick up on that. Amelia wasn't sure if that should be an important sign of something.

She set down her fork. "Livestock and equipment started going missing from some of the more prosperous ranches around town. Byron McKay—that grouch is the reason for my pie today, if you really want to know—was hit first. Ten head of cattle and a whole bunch of fancy equipment just walked off his ranch. You don't want to get on Byron's bad side, let me tell you. He's barely nice on a good day. Only it didn't stop there."

Finn started on the cherry pie. "The rustlers struck again?"

"They hit Carson Thorn's ranch. He's the head of our chapter of the Lone Star Cowboy League. That's a service organization that helps ranchers in these parts. Carson's as nice as they come, so then we knew it wasn't just someone sore at Byron. There have been over ten thefts since September alone, all different kinds of things taken from different kinds of ranches. Even the Welcome to Little Horn sign disappeared. It's got everyone more than a little spooked."

"So your perpetrators weren't all about personal retaliation."

Amelia saw Finn register the same surprise she felt at his choice of words. The technical language he used was the same she'd heard over and over from Lucy and from her ex-fiancé, Rafe. Police language.

So Finn's interest in the rustling likely wasn't criminal, it was professional. Her instincts *were* right, he *was* a good man. The satisfaction at her insight warred with the residual sting she still carried over men with badges. If that wasn't enough to warn her off the connection she felt with him—and it was—Finn's watch had told her someone was waiting for him to come home. Should she mention that?

She decided on a different topic instead. "You talk like you're with the law, Finn. Are you?"

His eyes squinted, trying the idea on for size. "Could be. Only wouldn't the force be out looking for me if I was? Dr. Searle says no one has filed a missing-persons report for anyone matching my description." He said the words with a weary acceptance that made Amelia's throat tighten.

"Of course someone's missing you. I've no doubt there's a pretty lady plain out of her mind with worry right now."

Finn put down his fork, the rest of the cherry pie uneaten. "I don't think so. I don't feel any sense that there's anyone out there missing me." His eyes lost all their warmth. Amelia had met plenty of people in tight spots but she couldn't remember ever seeing the kind of lifeless resignation that currently filled Finn's features. He looked as if it came as no surprise that no one missed him.

"Sure there is." She said it as much to remind herself as to remind him. "There's B."

"B?" Amelia spoke as if the letter should mean something to him, and Finn had the vaguest sensation that it did.

"Doc Searle didn't show you the watch?"

Finn looked at his left hand, noticing the now-faint tan line that showed where he wore his watch. Dr. Searle had mentioned an inscribed watch but hadn't shown it to him. Somewhere from the back of his brain came the fact that where a man wore his watch usually indicated if he was left-or right-handed. It seemed an odd detail for a person to know with the certainty he did and backed up the theory that he was somehow connected with law or security—he seemed used to collecting details as clues. Only if that were true, where was the force that should be out looking for their missing officer? Why wasn't someone posting departmental notices? APBs?

Finn went to reach for the small drawer in his bedside table, but the action sent jolts of pain through his chest. "Let me look," Amelia said.

"It's in here." She pulled out a square gold watch on a black leather band. A nice watch, the kind that got given as a gift. Amelia placed it face-down in Finn's hand. He ran one finger over the words as he read the inscription. *Finn: all my love, B.* The sight of those words brought up a bittersweet emotion he couldn't place. Sorrow? Regret? Loss? Anger? It wasn't clear enough to name, but it was strong enough to tighten his throat.

"See?" Amelia's soft, comforting voice came at his shoulder. "There's at least one person out there who loves you and misses you." She said it like a blessing, like something that should make him feel better. It didn't, but he couldn't explain why. His face must have shown the turmoil, for Amelia's face lost its encouraging glow and she backed away. "I'm sorry. Maybe there was a reason Dr. Searle waited to show that to you."

"No," Finn countered, "I'm glad you did...sort of. Kind of helps to see solid evidence that I'm Finn." He turned the watch over to stare at the face. It should look familiar, but it was just an object. "I was wearing this when you found me?" He knew plenty of men who'd stopped wearing watches now that cell phones were an easy way to keep track of time—the watch clearly had sentimental value to him.

"It's all we had to go on. There was no wallet or cell phone or car keys or that sort of thing."

"If it was a robbery, why not take the watch?" His brain was used to putting facts together like this—it made Finn more convinced he was in some kind of security field.

"That's what I can't figure out. Only, you were wearing gloves—I found the glove before I found you—so maybe they didn't see the watch." Amelia twisted a finger around one curl of her cascading blond hair, hesitating before asking, "So, no idea who B is?"

Finn took a deep breath, trying to focus his thoughts, to push them through the veil of murky nothingness. "Only that she's important." It surprised him—in a much-needed good way—that he knew B was a she. He felt like some strange emotional version of Hansel and Gretel, scanning the world for bits and pieces of a trail to lead him back home. He was Finn and he had—or once had—a B. It wasn't nearly enough to go on, but other than his recollections of Amelia's rescue, it was all he had.

He put the watch on, pleased to note it matched the faint tan line on his wrist. He had at least something of his life now. "Thanks for showing that to me. It helps. Really." He smiled at her, pleased when she smiled back.

"There is more, you know," Amelia said as she

rose up off the chair to open the narrow closet on the far side of the room. "You were wearing these when I found you." She held up a pair of jeans, a plaid shirt and a heavy fleece—clothes that could have been attributed to half the men in Texas, and certainly no big clues to his identity. "Nice boots," Amelia offered as she hoisted a pair of worn cowboy boots. She was digging for anything positive to bolster his spirits, and it touched him that she was trying so hard.

"They *look* like mine," he said, not sure how he could make the claim but wanting to go along with her relentless hunt for affirmations. "Like something I think I'd wear, I mean."

"Well," she said, rehanging the clothes, "you know more now than you did this morning. Tomorrow you'll find out even more. That's what Dr. Searle said, that you'd get things back as you went along. Why, I wouldn't be surprised if by this time tomorrow you know your name, your address and your grandmother's birthday."

A knock on the door signaled Dr. Searle's entry into the room. He nodded toward the watch on his hand. "So you've seen that. Bring up anything?"

Nothing good, but Finn didn't really want to admit that. "I don't know who B is, if that's what you're asking."

"Only it's a she, and she's important," Amelia added. "That's good progress, don't you think?"

Finn touched the watch again and thought about the tender inscription now against his skin. B sounded like a wife, or a sister, or a love—so why didn't he remember her, and why hadn't she come looking for him? Why was his response to the watch so dark? Nothing made any sense.

"Pie?" Dr. Searle noticed the three pieces sitting on the tray beside Finn's bed.

"Amelia was fixing to convert me to her theory that pie makes everything better. And that knowing which flavors I like was vital information."

Dr. Searle laughed. "I could think of worse therapies."

"I read that tastes and smells are among the most powerful memories. It seemed like an ideal way to wake up Finn's brain cells."

Finn sat up. "You were researching amnesia?" He hated using that term to refer to whatever it was that happened to him. It sounded so dramatic.

"Well, if you call looking things up on the internet on your smartphone while you're waiting in line at the pharmacy for Gramps's prescriptions research, then yes. I mean, really, how many amnesia patients does a person get to meet? It's fascinating."

Not so much from where I sit, Finn thought darkly. The feeling of everything being just slightly beyond his control was too prickly for his liking. Exhaustion pulled on his composure, and he tried to stifle a yawn.

"Speaking of Gramps, I'd better get home to him. He's usually good about his evening medicines, but not always. And he's an absolute bear in the morning if he stays up too late watching television." She touched Finn's arm again in that soft, kind way. "You must be worn-out—it's been quite a day. I expect rest is about the best gift you can give yourself right now, so see that you get lots of it. I'll stop back by tomorrow after church. And I've already added you to the prayer list, so you're set there."

"Pie, pajamas and prayer—what more can a man ask for?" Finn had to wonder if he was always this bad at conversation or if his slumbering synapses just made him say stupid things. "Thank you," he offered, finding the words painfully inadequate for all Amelia Klondike had done.

Her blue eyes glowed, as if she understood all he'd failed to say. "You're welcome. Rest up now, and we'll see what else comes back to you tomorrow." Amelia collected her things and sent him one last warm look before ducking out the door.

"Is she really that nice to everybody?" Finn asked Dr. Searle as they heard her heels clip down the hallway.

"Amelia? Sure thing. Helping people is what Amelia does. Ever since she and her sister came into her daddy's money, she's turned helping folks into a full-time thing. Me, I might have skedaddled to some tropical island with that kind of cash, but Amelia just turned her hobby into a nonstop kindness campaign. My wife says Amelia would just about up and die if she had to stop giving folks a hand up—it's her gift." He motioned for Finn's wrist and took his pulse. "If I had to pick anyone in Little Horn to find me out cold in the woods, it'd be Amelia. God was watching out for you, son. You remember that when all this memory nonsense gets to you."

"It'll come back, won't it, Doc?"

Dr. Searle sat down on the chair Amelia had vacated. "It should. The brain is the organ we know the least about—lots of it is still a mystery. But amnesia onset by head trauma is less rare than you think. You may never remember the accident, but the rest of it is likely to come back over the next few days."

Finn fiddled with the thin hospital gown, suddenly eager to get into pajamas like a normal person instead of this ridiculous getup that made him feel like an invalid. "Do I have to stay in here until it does?"

"Your preliminary tests will be done by tomorrow afternoon, and then come back for an office visit Monday. So yes, you'll be free to go tomorrow but, Finn, *where* would you go?"

If Finn was supposed to get rest, there wasn't a less restful question in all the world.

Chapter Three

I should never have agreed to this. Finn stared at the holiday decorations that filled Amelia Klondike's front porch late Sunday afternoon and fought the urge to bolt for the nearest hotel. As grateful as he was to get out of the hospital, *their* annoying holiday decorations paled in comparison to the blast of Christmas cheer that was Amelia's house.

Why did anything Christmas bother him so? It was something else to heap onto the pile of unknowns. Dr. Searle had showed him a list of missing-persons reports, but none of them contained a Finn and he still couldn't even say if Finn was a first, last or nickname. It made obscure recollections like his intense dislike of Christmas that much harder to bear. Finn knew he didn't like any of it, but he still didn't know why.

"You don't need to put me up, Amelia. I don't

want to put you and your grandfather out." The fact that he hadn't seen anything even close to a motel on the short drive from the hospital just made it worse.

"Nonsense. Where else would you go with no wallet, no credit cards and no name other than Finn?"

Thanks, he thought, *it sounds so much less desperate when you put it that way.*

He must not have hidden his scowl well. "Even if you knew your address—" Amelia backpedaled "—you're not supposed to drive. You can't possibly live nearby, so how would you come back for those tests Doc Searle wants? And to tell the truth—" she gave him one of her wide-eyed, I-can't-help-myself-from-helping looks "—I just plain think you shouldn't be left on your own." She pulled her silver SUV into the garage. "Gramps loves a mystery and no one even uses the upstairs bedrooms anymore. Besides, even if there was a hotel in town, what if some traumatic accident memory comes back to you in the middle of the night? Who'd want that in some cold hotel room all alone? I couldn't forgive myself if I let that happen."

One fact had become relentlessly clear: trying to stop Amelia Klondike from lending a hand to a soul she thought in need was like trying to stop a buffalo stampede with a flyswatter. It couldn't be done—not without getting trampled. *It won't be for long*, Finn told himself. *Things are coming back to you. It'd be rude to refuse, right? She's been so nice.* From out of nowhere, Finn got the sense that he hadn't had much home comfort of late—a vague impression of microwave bachelor food and bare-bones furniture pushed its way into his consciousness. He shivered—as if his body remembered the cold of the place without his brain remembering where that place was.

"What was that?"

Finn blinked, pulling himself back from the—the what? Memory? Hunch?—to see Amelia staring at him with a startled concern in her eyes. "What was what?" he asked, knowing that would do nothing to stave off her questioning.

She cut the car's ignition. "Your whole face changed just now. And you shivered. You remembered something, didn't you?"

It bothered him that she could see it. He wanted the return of his memories to be private. He was a private person—that much he knew. "I'm not sure." It was no lie—he wasn't sure what that flash in his brain was. "Except I think I live alone. And…not very well."

Her voice changed, going all soft and warm in a way that got under his skin. "What did you just remember?"

He didn't want to tell her, but the image rattled

so loudly in his head it had to come out. "When you said that about waking up alone in the dark upset. I've done that. Or used to do that. A lot."

"Oh, Finn. Do you know why?" Her eyes were so bittersweet, as if she knew exactly how it felt to be alone in the dark missing someone.

Missing someone? Where had that come from? Was it B? Was B gone from his life, whomever she was? Was that why no one was looking for him?

He caught her eyes again, feeling unmoored and too much at the mercy of randomly returning memories. He shifted his eyes to his hands and willed his fingers to unclench from their white-knuckled curl. "I don't think I was a very happy man." He wanted to take back the words the moment they escaped. To not know so much but to know *that*? What kind of torture was it going to be like to have things trickle back like this? "I don't like Christmas." He needed her to know how hard this was right now. Everything was messed up—he wanted company and he needed to be alone. He needed to remember but didn't like what was coming back to him.

She blinked at him, unable to accept the thought. "Everybody likes Christmas."

"I didn't. I don't. I mean…" Finn blew out a breath, the exhaustion welling up over him again. "I don't know what I mean."

"I'm sure I can't begin to imagine what you are going through. It's got to be so hard. But if there's anything I do know, Finn, it's that hard things are harder alone." The dark, hard edge showed in the corners of her eyes again, the way it had whenever they talked about the possibility of him being in law enforcement. He'd noticed that little detail like he'd noticed a dozen others—how she avoided talking about herself, how she curled a finger around her hair when she got nervous, how everyone spoke about her in tones of veiled "bless her heart" pity.

Maybe that was why he felt such an affinity for her; she'd been knocked down by something but was fighting to stay up. He wasn't very good at that fight but she was; she hadn't let whatever it was beat her down. Maybe it wouldn't be so bad to let a bit of that optimism rub off on him.

A wedge of light spilled on the car, and Finn looked up to see an older man standing in the door that led to the house. He could see more Christmas decorations behind the man, even from here. The urge to run was as strong as the urge to go inside. Not knowing quite who he was seemed to push every emotion closer to the surface, and he was too tired to fight it.

"Come inside," Amelia coaxed. "If you still want to leave in the morning, we'll talk about it. It's almost supper and you need food and rest."

The scents of a home kitchen wafted through the garage as he hauled himself out of the car and Finn's stomach growled. He winced as he grabbed the tiny "luggage" the hospital had given him—sad to note all his current possessions fit into the small plastic bag.

"Finn, is it?" called the old man, leaning on a cane. He had Amelia's eyes and a head full of bushy gray hair.

"Yes, sir."

The man waved the formality off. "Oh, don't 'sir' me. Luther'll be just fine." He held out a hand with thick, wrinkled fingers and shook Finn's with a strong grip. "Tough go you've had there, son. I could barely believe it when Amelia told me." He hobbled into the kitchen, motioning for Finn to follow.

A holiday home decor tidal wave assaulted Finn's eyes, bringing a surge of nauseated panic to clutch at Finn's throat.

"It gets worse every year," Luther remarked, his expression telling Finn that he hadn't hid his reaction well. "I feel like I'm living in a department store window some days."

Pine boughs, candy canes and red ribbon seemed to erupt from every available surface. A miniature tree with tiny ornaments stood in the center of the kitchen table while lights twinkled from every window.

Amelia bustled in behind him, her face a mix of pride and embarrassment given the admission he'd just made in the car. "I admit," she said with a raised eyebrow, "I enjoy the holidays."

"I think we went past 'enjoy' four years ago." Luther gave Amelia an indulgent kiss on the cheek. "Now it's closer to 'obsess.' Gets it from her mother, God rest her soul."

Amelia set another bakery box down on the counter—more experimental pie slices?—and shucked off her coat. "Gramps says all the Klondike men married women with the gift for ornamentation."

The gift for ornamentation. That was one way to put it. Finn fished for some kind of well-mannered compliment to pay the display, but came up short. When the kitchen clock struck the hour by playing "Joy to the World," he wanted to shut his eyes and run from the room. But what good would that do? The rest of the house would likely offer the same festive assault.

A series of snuffles and small barks came from another part of the house, and a fat dog with bulging eyes waddled into the room.

"Bug, say hello to our new friend Finn."

Bug, who looked as if his face was permanently pushed up against some invisible glass window, sniffed noisily around Finn's boots, a pig-curly tail twitching in curiosity. Finn reached down and let the dog sniff his hand. "Hi there, Bug." Bug, of course, sported a red collar dotted with green Christmas trees and a shiny silver bell.

Bug's interest in Finn lasted only until Amelia lifted the lid off a Crock-Pot on the counter, sending a spicy, beefy aroma into the air. That sent Bug to jumping at Amelia's feet, hoping for a taste. Finn couldn't blame the dog for his enthusiasm. Real food. Maybe he could put up with the Yuletide high tide if it came with good home cooking. He owed it to himself—and to Amelia—to at least try.

"Dinner will be ready in about fifteen minutes. Gramps, why don't you show Finn to his room and he can settle in."

"Less decorations up there, I think," Luther said as he headed for a banister wrapped in red and gold ribbon. "You're upstairs at the end of the hall. I don't do stairs anymore, so I'll just point you in the right direction, if that's okay." He pointed to a door Finn could just see off the left of the staircase. "Take a moment to wash up and get your bearings, and we'll see you back down here in just a bit."

"Thanks, Luther." Finn mounted the first stair, then found himself reaching for the banister. His side was throbbing, and he didn't like the fact that he needed the support to climb the flight.

"Think nothing of it, son. Least we can do."

Nobody has to do anything for me, Finn thought darkly. *I've no friends here.*

That's not true, a small voice argued with his darker nature. *And that's not bad.*

"Are you sure this is a good idea?" Amelia didn't like the scowl Lucy Benson gave her as they took Bug for his evening walk when Lucy stopped over after supper. "I know you can't help helping," Lucy continued, "but we don't know anything about him. For all we know he could be connected to the thefts."

Amelia buttoned up her coat against the evening chill. "He's not a criminal, Lucy."

"Amelia, you don't know that. Seeing the good in everybody doesn't mean you have to put them up in your home. He could rob you blind while you sleep tonight and it's not as if you and Gramps and Bug could defend yourselves."

Amelia stopped walking to stare at Lucy. "He's not our rustler, Lucy. I'm sure of it."

"Well, forgive me if I don't put that much stock in those hunches of yours. Being sheriff means I have to depend more on solid evidence than your famous intuition."

Amelia chose a new topic. "Well, Madam Sheriff, what new have you learned about our cattle thieves? Any closer to catching whoever is doing all this?" Little Horn had been experiencing a strange brand of crime spree, with cattle disappearing from wealthy ranchers' estates while gifts of supplies and equipment had appeared to families in need. A cowboy version of Robin Hood.

"Some folks are downright scared, having their security violated and goods stolen. And they've a right to be worried. I don't mind telling you I'm getting a lot of pressure to solve this case. The finger-pointing is going to get ugly if we don't get a break soon." Lucy pushed out a sigh, her breath a white whisp in the clear night air. "Then there are the folks who've received gifts. They're grateful, but I know they can't help thinking their gain might be at someone else's expense. As to who's doing it? I wish I knew." She gave Amelia a sideways glance. "And I can't say your fellow isn't involved, Amelia. Have you thought about that he may be involved and not remember it? With this amnesia thing, he could genuinely believe he was innocent and still be guilty."

Amelia hadn't thought of that. "I can see that all of his memories aren't happy ones. There's something dark just beyond his reach—he's even said as much—but it can't be criminal. He uses phrases you do, which makes me think he's in law enforcement."

Lucy stopped walking and halted Amelia with a hand on her shoulder. "All the more reason for you to steer clear. I get that he's handsome and in distress and all, but haven't you sworn off us badge types since Rafe?"

"I'm helping him, not dating him, Lucy."

"And what if one turns into the other?"

"Believe me, I won't let it." Bug pulled on the leash, in no mood to stand still on such a chilly night. "I trust the nudges I get to help somebody." Amelia started walking again. "God's never sent me astray yet, and I don't think He's gonna start now. Finn needs a whopping load of grace and a safe place to work everything through. I don't think it's any surprise to God that I'm the one who found him—I'm the one who was *supposed* to find him. I *can* help, so I'm *going* to help."

"I'm not saying don't help him. I'm saying don't *take him in*."

"He needs *taking in* most of all. You said it yourself—there's no one looking for him. Can you imagine how that feels? He's the worst kind of lonely. I can't let him go through that in some hotel two towns over, not when Gramps and I are here and we've got the room and I'm the one who found him."

"Well, I've been your friend long enough to know you're gonna do this no matter what I say." This wasn't the first time Amelia had listened to a lecture from Lucy on overextending her helpful nature. She reminded herself that a friend who spoke the truth in love was a good friend to have, even when it felt exasperating. "Just promise me you'll be careful, and you'll listen if I have to come to you with information you don't like."

"Fair enough. And if Finn remembers anything I think you should hear, I promise I'll tell you. Even if it proves my hunch is wrong." She narrowed an eye at Lucy. "But it never is."

"Yet," Lucy corrected, wagging a finger at Amelia.

"Yet," Amelia conceded. She was glad to feel the tension leave the conversation. "But really, have you got any leads at all?"

Lucy squared her shoulders. "The League Rustling Investigation Team and I have a theory or two."

"Any you can share?" Amelia tried to be sensitive to Lucy's official capacity and the sensitive information that often went with it.

"There's a ranch hand, someone with a sketchy past who worked at three of the big ranches that got hit. He'd know the layout enough to get in and pull off the burglaries."

"That seems like a strong lead." Amelia loved to watch Lucy work on a case. She was an amazing strategist, a talented puzzle-solver who could see connections others missed. Little Horn was blessed to have her.

"There's more," Lucy went on. "This same guy

just won a handful in the state lottery. That would puff him up enough to dare taking revenge on any ranch that let him go."

"And it would mean he'd have the funds to give gifts to the struggling ranchers," Amelia added. "I know you were wondering how our thief was turning all that livestock and equipment into cash for those other purchases so quickly." It wasn't as if a saddle went missing from one ranch only to appear on another—the taken items seemed to disappear, while different gifted items showed up out of nowhere.

"Only, I can't connect him to the folks who've gotten gifts yet, only the folks who were robbed."

"You'll find the connection. You always do. And you've got the 'Posse' helping you."

Lucy rolled her eyes at the nickname some of the townspeople had given the Rustling Investigation Team. "'Helping' isn't always helpful. I had to make Tom Horton give me his gun on our stakeout the other night—he's a little too eager to play 'cops and robbers' if you ask me. I'm glad to have Doc Grainger and Carson join the team, but we're still not getting anywhere solid. Byron's demanding answers, and he's not alone."

Byron McKay had been the first and hardest hit, so he had cause to be concerned. Only, Byron was tough to like under even the best of circumstances. He'd been mean to everyone lately, so

Amelia could just imagine the kind of grief Byron must be giving Lucy for the fact that the identity of Little Horn's ranch brand of Robin Hood remained unsolved. "Byron making your life miserable?"

"More than usual, and that's saying something." Lucy let out a weary sigh. "If we don't solve this soon it's going to be a hard, mean Christmas in Little Horn."

Her friend's words brought the ice from Finn's eyes back to Amelia's memory. Had Finn known nothing but hard, mean Christmases? Surely Little Horn could change that. Surely she, of all people, could change that.

Chapter Four

Monday while Finn was back at Dr. Searle's for more tests and treatments, Amelia went to visit her younger sister, Lizzie, to go over plans for Lizzie's upcoming wedding. As she watched her sister slump onto the couch, Amelia would be hard-pressed to say who was having the more trying afternoon—her or Finn. "I'm tired of all this," Lizzie moaned, hand on her forehead "Why do we have to plan everything so far in advance?"

Lizzie's wedding plans couldn't be classified as 'far in advance' by any stretch of the imagination. As much as she loved putting together events, and Lizzie really was the only family she had other than Gramps, Amelia was starting to regret her role as stand-in mother of the bride/wedding planner. "You want it to come off well, don't you? You keep telling me you want the perfect wedding."

"I do." Lizzie sighed, gesturing to the stack of wedding magazines and notes scattered across the coffee table. "I want Boone and my wedding to be spectacular."

"Well—" Amelia tried to keep the frustration from her voice "—spectacular can't really be done at the last minute. It's December, and you want to get married the first weekend in April. You've got a whole lot of great ideas here. You just need to make a few decisions." She leaned in and gave Lizzie a supportive nudge. "Settling on a color scheme would go a long way to getting us organized."

Lizzie sunk her face in her hands. "Ugh. I can't decide. You choose."

Amelia pulled out the three color schemes. It had taken her two weeks just to get Lizzie to narrow it down to three. "I am not choosing your color scheme for you. I'll happily implement it down to the last detail, but honey, this is your and Boone's wedding. You and Boone need to make some of the decisions." Secretly, Amelia knew which she was rooting for—and it wasn't the purple and sage. And the red and gold was just too bold no matter how she looked at it. No, the mint and cream was by far the best for Lizzie's skin tone and the early-spring timing. *It's not my place to choose*, she reminded herself even as her hand rested on the mint-and-cream palette. *Don't over-help. This needs to be Lizzie's choice.*

"Boone told me I could do whatever I wanted."

Amelia had heard enough do-whatever-you-wants from Rafe to recognize such disinterest as a red flag between couples. Still, she could just as easily suspect Boone to be nothing more than frustrated with Lizzie's indecision. "Well, then, it really is up to you. They're all fine choices, Lizzie, just pick one."

Lizzie straightened on the couch. Amelia wished she believed in mental telepathy so she could send *Mint, mint, mint!* messages to her sister. As it was, she just said a prayer for wisdom on Lizzie's part and grace for herself.

"I want the red and gold. I want lots of shiny gold details so my wedding sparkles."

Not exactly a spring palette—more holiday, to tell the truth—but at least Lizzie had chosen. "Excellent choice. You'll have the sparkliest wedding in the county. I can see red roses and gold ribbons in your bouquet already, can't you?"

Lizzie's eyes fairly glowed as she picked up the paper with all the red-gold color variations on it. "You know what I was thinking, Lia?" Lizzie often used the nickname she'd given her sister when as a youngster she couldn't quite pronounce Amelia.

"I was thinking I'd love to walk down the aisle

in sparkly gold shoes. I'd feel like a princess in glittery shoes. And Boone's vest could be gold lamé, couldn't it?"

Amelia swallowed the *disco ball* remark tickling the tip of her tongue and smiled. "There's all kinds of things we can do now that you've made your choice." She slid the elegant mint-and-cream pages back into her file alongside the purple and sage. If Lizzie wanted to shout her color scheme to the world, that was a bride's choice. She'd just have to do a big sister's best to ensure the wedding guests didn't feel as if they'd run off to the circus. Amelia hid the grin such a thought gave her behind a sip of iced tea.

"Can we rent a tent?" Lizzie asked, shifting the gold fabric on the paper this way and that to catch the sunshine coming in through the windows.

The circus-tent connection was a bit too striking, and Amelia nearly choked on her tea. "Pardon?"

"Do you think we can have the wedding outside under a tent?"

"April can be a bit unpredictable weather-wise, Lizzie. We might want to stick with the League banquet hall to keep things from becoming a circus." She cringed at the word choice, fighting the urge to whack her own forehead.

"A circus!" Lizzie's eyes went wide. "That's it!"

That is not it. Oh, please, don't let that be it. "Oh, Lizzie, I'm not so sure that's a…"

Lizzie had already shot up off the couch, circling the room with animated gestures. "Can't you see it? A circus wedding? No one would ever forget it!"

I can guarantee you that, Amelia thought. "Lizzie, honey…"

"Couldn't you just see Boone in one of those red coats? The ones with the black lapels? And a top hat? Just like one of those—" she whirled a hand, trying to pick the word out of the air "—what are they called?"

Amelia began to feel slightly ill. "Ringmaster?" Her voice took on an unfortunate squeak with the word.

Lizzie spread her hands in delight, oblivious to Amelia's alarm. "Exactly. Oh, Lia, you're right—it *is* the perfect choice. You're so good at this. I'm so glad you're my sister." She bent over Amelia and hugged her tight. "If anyone can give me a circus wedding, it's you!"

"Sure." Amelia winced inside her sister's hug. "You know me and parties."

Lizzie released her and began pushing papers around on the coffee table in search of her cell phone. "I've just got to tell Boone right away!" She punched in a few numbers and then practically skipped off to the kitchen to leave Amelia staring at the red-and-gold carnage scattered across the table. "Guess what, Pookie?" Lizzie shouted from the other room, using the ridiculous nickname she and Boone continually used. Amelia put a finger to the bridge of her nose and exhaled slowly. *You wanted her to choose. At least everything red and gold should be on sale right after Christmas.*

She would swallow the cringe she suspected would permanently settle in her stomach and give Lizzie a wonderful wedding, because she was the only one who could. Mama's illness had taken her from Amelia and Lizzie when they were teenagers, so there was no mother of the bride to step in and help. Daddy had made sure she and Lizzie were very well provided for before his liver disease finally took him, but Amelia had always suspected Daddy died more of a broken heart than a sick liver. She had memories—good ones—of what Mama and Daddy had been like as a happy couple, but she could easily recall the light that never came back to Daddy's eyes once Mama was gone. Lizzie, being younger, maybe didn't have as many memories of their parents' marital bliss. That could be what was driving Lizzie's urges for a nuptial spectacular.

Or—and Amelia felt a shudder at the thought—the urge to prove that at least one Klondike could make it to the altar.

And really, was it such a chore to give her baby sister the wedding of her dreams? *More like saving Lizzie from herself,* Amelia mused, picturing what Lizzie's unrestrained imagination could dream up. Left to her own devices, Lizzie might rent an elephant to give rides on the League front lawn. *Oh, Lord, I'm gonna need a heap of grace and patience for this. And you know I don't have much of either on this particular subject.*

"Boone just loved the idea!" Lizzie came back into the room to plop down on the couch, arms and legs skewed at dramatic angles. "People will be talking about this wedding for years, don't you think?"

"Oh, I completely agree." One thing was sure—Lizzie's "circus" wedding would give Little Horn's wagging tongues something else to talk about than her own broken engagement. Amelia came over to sit next to Lizzie on the couch. "Just promise me one thing, baby sister."

"Sure. Anything."

Amelia took Lizzie's hand. "Promise me you'll put as much work into the marriage as you do into the wedding."

Lizzie pulled away the slightest bit. "What's that supposed to mean?"

"It means you and Boone are young. You haven't known each other all that long, and I haven't seen either of you in church for weeks.

A marriage is a lot more than just a fabulous party. If Daddy were here, he'd tell you a happy marriage takes hard work. I want you and Boone to have a happy marriage."

Lizzie pulled her hand from Amelia's. "You don't really like him, do you?"

Amelia sighed. They'd had some version of this discussion so many times. "I don't really know him. I want to get to know him, but I can hardly find ten minutes together with the two of you. He stayed all of thirty minutes at Thanksgiving."

"Boone had to be somewhere. Why are you coming down so hard on him?"

She'd never heard Boone talk of any nearby family—who had "places to be" on Thanksgiving? Places that didn't welcome the woman he intended to marry? "I'm not saying he's a bad choice, Lizzie. I'm just saying…"

"Oh, I get loud and clear what you're saying." Lizzie stood up. "Look, just because your fiancé left you high and dry doesn't mean every man is a louse."

"That's not at all what I mean."

Lizzie spun to turn on Amelia with sharp, narrow eyes. "Why can't you just let me be happy?"

"I do want you to be happy, Lizzie. And the right man will make you happy. Just give me a chance to get to know Boone as the right man."

"Boone *is* the right man for me. And if you

can't see that, maybe you shouldn't be helping with my wedding." Lizzie began stuffing all the notes back into the bag until Amelia put a hand out to stop her.

"I'm sorry. I trust you to choose the right man for you. But I wouldn't be your sister if I didn't try to counsel you toward a good marriage. Just promise me you and Boone will do the premarital program at church between now and April. Their isn't a soul on earth who doesn't need God's help to make a strong marriage. Even Daddy and Gramps would tell you that."

"Well—" Amelia was glad to see Lizzie sink back down onto the couch "—I have heard good things about Pastor Mathers's program. And I know Boone says he's okay with church."

Okay with church? Amelia wondered. *What kind of commitment is that?* "Then why don't you and Boone come to supper some night next week?"

"We'll see," Lizzie replied, holding the shiny gold fabric up to the light again.

We will indeed, Amelia thought to herself.

Dr. Searle waved the annoying flashlight again, peering too close at Finn. The bright light hurt. "So," the doctor said, trying too hard to sound casual, "anything new come back to you?"

"Vague impressions, but nothing useful. Nothing like my name, or my address, or what I do, or why I'm here." The list was depressing.

"Well, now, it hasn't been that long." Searle cued Finn to go through the silly-feeling exercises he had done at every visit—things like pushing and pulling against the doctor's grip. Physically, he was healing as well as could be expected. His brain wasn't being nearly as cooperative. "Still dizzy?" the doctor asked.

"Only if I stand up too fast or move my head too quickly. And when I'm tired. Which seems to be a lot." Finn was no fan of having to recite his current weaknesses. It was good to be out of the hospital, but he still felt like an invalid.

"All to be expected." Searle made some notations on a chart. "For what it's worth, I think it's a smart choice to be at Amelia's. You ought not to be on your own for the next few days, given that you're a fall risk."

That pronouncement sank into Finn's gut. Old people were fall risks, not him.

Searle raised an eyebrow. "You don't want to end up back here, do you?"

Had he been that irritable in the hospital? "No, sir." Searle's expression told Finn he hadn't been a dream patient.

Searle took off his glasses. "And I realize this may seem like asking a lot, but I'd like you to stay off the internet. We have Lucy and the sheriff's office working on your identity. You fishing around cyberspace for clues isn't the best use of your energies right now. The last thing you need is some false piece of information sending you down a stressful rabbit hole."

That seemed unreasonable. "But..."

Searle cut him off. "I understand this is uncomfortable for you. But, son, you're going to have to trust the healing process. Think of it this way—right now, your brain knows more than you do. It's going to give up secrets at a pace we can't determine. Force things, and you may end up making it worse for yourself. You're in no danger, you've got Amelia helping you—which means you've got all of Little Horn in your corner—so I see no reason to rush this."

Can an amnesiac fire his neurologist? Finn didn't much care for the advice he was getting, but even he knew there weren't other options at the moment. He was stuck in the here and now whether he liked it or not. "I hate this," he pointed out, petulant as it sounded.

"I can understand how you do. But the sooner you make peace with it, the better off you'll be."

I'm stuck in a small town with the Queen of Christmas and no idea who I am or how to get home, Finn thought darkly. *Right now I got a pretty low bar for "better off."*

Chapter Five

Amelia had just enough time after her visit with Lizzie to look in on poor Ben Stillwater and say a prayer for the still-unconscious young man. It reminded her that there were worse problems than questionable weddings. And speaking of worse problems, one look at Finn's face outside Dr. Searle's office told Amelia that clearly she hadn't had the worst afternoon of the day. The frustrated knot of Finn's eyebrows made him look years older than when she'd dropped him off before Lizzie's.

"That bad?" she asked.

"He made me do eye exercises that made me sick and dizzy. He told me I'm a 'fall risk' and to be patient and stay off the internet." Finn growled and headed straight for the door. "What's wrong with me that I can't sit in a chair and move my eyes without falling over?"

She hurried to keep up with his long strides. "You had a serious knock to your head, Finn. A concussion and all. That's going to take time to heal. You *are* going to have to be patient."

Finn gave her a look that displayed how little patience he had.

She was almost afraid to ask, "Any breakthroughs?"

"He showed me the list of missing-persons reports from the sheriff's office to see if any of the names felt familiar."

It didn't take Lucy's skills to guess the answer. "Nothing rang a bell?"

"I could be any of those people and not know it. I'm useless to find even my own name on a list." He furrowed one hand in his thick brown hair as if he could squeeze the answers out with his fingers.

Amelia knew stress wasn't helpful in his situation, but she had no idea how to calm Finn down. "Well, he did say none of the missing-persons reports matched your description, so isn't it possible your name wasn't on that list?"

He stopped walking to glare at her. "Yes. No one is out there looking for me. I've dropped off the face of the earth and no one has even noticed. You can imagine how comforting that is."

Amelia had spent the better part of last year wanting to disappear. Here was a man who actually had, and he was twelve times more miserable than she'd ever been. *There's a lesson in that, Lord. Thank You. But help me help him.* "I can imagine how lonely that must be. I'm glad you're staying with us and not going through this by yourself. I'm glad to help you, however I can."

"There isn't anything you can do, Amelia." He stuffed his hands into his pockets and resumed walking toward the car. "There isn't a solution for this."

She grabbed his jutting elbow, stopping him again. "That's because the solution for this is time. You just need to hang on until the first bits of memory come back—and they will."

His eyes were so sad. "How do you know they will?"

She didn't, of course, but she refused to believe he'd be living under the weight of a blank slate forever. "I just do. My intuition is legendary, you know."

He didn't exactly roll his eyes, but his face was far from confident. *Hopeless* was a better word, and it jabbed into her chest.

"You didn't die out there in the woods. You're alive and healing. I just came from visiting a young man named Ben Stillwater in that same medical center. He fell from his horse and is in a coma, not walking around like you are. You've a lot to be thankful for, Finn, and maybe you'd be better off focusing on all you have instead of parts you've lost." She hadn't planned a lecture, but someone had to shake him out of this harmful dark funk. "Why, Gramps would give his eye teeth to have your strength. Even Bug is jealous of how you can walk up the stairs."

That almost made him laugh. "Your dog is jealous of me?"

"Haven't you seen him standing at the bottom of the stairs looking up toward your room? He used to love to sleep in the sun in that room, and now he can't make it up there. I've seen him watch you when you go up. He's jealous."

He narrowed his eyes at her, but at least now it was more in puzzlement than anger. "And this is supposed to make me feel better?"

"I admit, it's not a tidal wave of encouragement, but…"

He shook his head. "You amaze me. No one else would ever come up with a fat dog's envy as a source of encouragement."

"Bug is not fat."

Finn gave her a you've-got-to-be-kidding-me look.

"Okay, maybe Bug could stand to shed a few pounds."

That incredulous look only deepened. If he was in law enforcement, he had the intimidating eyes for it.

"Maybe more than a few. Look, you know what I'm trying to say here. Count your blessings—that's all you can do in a situation like this." She sighed, her own frustration getting the better of her. "With a sister like Lizzie, it's all either of us can do."

"Things not go well with your sister today?"

Amelia spilled the whole story of Lizzie's wedding theme. The weight of having to be her ever-helpful self lifted as she watched his reaction. At least *someone* else found Lizzie's ideas quirky if not downright odd. He balked at the ringmaster-coat idea, and she was glad for both their sakes of his genuine laugh at her worries that Lizzie might rent an elephant.

"See," she said as she unlocked the car, "the best antidote for your own troubles is to help someone else with theirs."

He eased himself into the car with a wince; his ribs evidently still hurt him. "I haven't done a thing to help you with any of that."

"Yes, you have. You listened. And you laughed, so I know I'm not the only one who thinks this whole thing is crazy."

"Anyone with any sense at all would laugh at that crazy idea."

She pointed a teasing finger at him. "Don't you dare say that in front of Lizzie."

"Sure, boss, whatever you say."

Before she put the car in gear, she gave Finn a direct look. "Am I right, do you feel better? Even the tiniest bit?"

His boyish grin was all too charming. "Sort of."

"Well, you look less like Scrooge than you did ten minutes ago. That's got to count for something." The tension had eased in his shoulders, and most of his scowl was gone. Stealing a glance while she pulled the car out of the parking lot, Amelia wondered what Finn would look like happy. He was a handsome sort even down-and-out—all that dark glossy hair and those stunning blue eyes made brooding a good look on his features. Well and happy, she didn't doubt he'd be a heart-slayer. Based on what she'd already seen, if Finn revived confidence, he'd command a room.

If they could retrieve one tiny detail. The article she'd read said taste, smell and music had some of the most powerful abilities to reawaken brain functions. People who couldn't manage speech could often sing. Alzheimer's patients who couldn't recall their spouses could remember how to play instruments. The trouble was, most of the tastes and scents and sounds around them now were about Christmas, and that was as much of a hindrance as a help for Finn. They'd already used a gift card provided by the hospital to get Finn some basics like a few changes of clothes and soap. There must be something on her to-do list that Finn could help her accomplish.

"We're going to the candy store. Is that okay?"

"Candy?"

"I have to buy candy to fill the stockings for the League Christmas party. I want the good stuff, not just anything from the supermarket. Can you help?" He looked a bit tired, but she didn't think sitting at home with Gramps watching game shows was going to do him any good, either.

"Is this another of your 'let's find things you like' experiments?"

She chose his earlier response. "Sort of. I mean, you might. But I really do need to get this done and I really could use the help."

"Don't you have to get home to Luther?"

She liked that he had taken to Gramps. They were good for each other in a way she couldn't quite yet explain. "We'll be home by suppertime easily. And quite frankly, if I have to tell Gramps his granddaughter is planning a circus wedding, I want some of his favorite butterscotch to soften the blow. And I always give a big basket of candy to Lucy and the sheriff's office every Christmas, so we can take care of that, too." She hesitated a moment before asking, "Do you still feel like maybe you are in some kind of law-enforcement field?"

Finn settled back in his seat. "As much as I

know anything. Only it doesn't help much. Texas could have thousands of law-enforcement officers my age and height. Police, private security, Rangers, FBI—without a name there's no good way to search."

"Can't they run *Finn*?"

"Dr. Searle had someone try. It's unusual enough that it would pop, but nothing. We both think it's a nickname, but that's no help, either."

"Something will come back to you. Or we'll find some detail that leads us to another. You've got to keep your hope strong."

"And you think butterscotch is the key to that?" He managed a small smile at that, and she was glad for it.

"Well, no, but I don't see how it could hurt."

"What kind of a fool scheme is that?" Luther waved the serving spoon in the air so hard at dinner that night that Finn fought the urge to duck away from airborne mashed potatoes. Amelia had elected to wait until dinner to reveal Lizzie's crazy wedding plans, which Finn thought as good a strategy as any.

He wasn't sure it worked. Luther's reaction to the circus theme was just about as stunned as Finn's own response. Amelia had laid it out in even greater detail than she had to him. A regrettable choice, he thought—it only got worse with the elaboration.

"My granddaughter's getting married at a circus?" Luther balked.

"A circus-*themed* wedding. There's a difference." Amelia was trying to champion Lizzie's absurd idea, but if Finn could see right through Amelia's forced support, surely Luther could, as well.

"Not how I see it." Luther snorted. Finn sent Amelia a "hang in there" look. "Why on earth didn't you stop her?"

"She couldn't choose a color scheme to save her life. Somehow when I said the word *circus*, it all just clicked for her." Finn watched Amelia run a fork through her potatoes, the air of a doomed woman coming through her false smile. "Believe me, it wasn't my intent to suggest an actual circus *at all*. She latched on to the idea, and evidently Boone loves it. Lizzie wants it to be memorable."

"She'll get her wish," Finn offered, "but I don't think it will turn out the way she wants."

"It won't be so awful." Amelia's voice pitched up in such a way that no one in the room—probably not even Bug—believed that to be true.

"Darlin'—" Luther leaned in "—you'd best rein that girl in something fierce or no Klondike in the county will be able to hold their head up for years." His words were heavy but Finn had to give the old man credit; there was still a teasing twinkle in his eyes. Finn guessed he'd grouse and balk but end up standing behind his granddaughter no matter what she chose.

"Gramps, we *are* the only Klondikes in the county."

"All the more reason to uphold the family name."

There was a pause in conversation while everyone tried to get their minds around the impending drama. Finn felt ungraciously glad to be a temporary guest of the family. Lizzie planned to be married in the spring. He ought to be long gone to his regular life by then, misfiring brain cells or not.

"We may never live it down." Resignation dropped Luther's words to a sigh.

A storm of gray swept over Amelia's eyes. "Well, Gramps, it's not like Klondikes and weddings have a stellar track record."

Whatever that remark meant, it stopped any further conversation cold, leaving Finn to make a mental note to investigate further. The look that passed between Amelia and Luther told him there was a story behind that comment, and it wasn't a happy one. What could possibly put so big a dent in Amelia Klondike's unshakable optimism?

He found his chance to ask while he and Amelia did the dishes after supper. Luther snoozed in the den under his usual pretense of watching the television news. It was a quiet time in the house Finn especially enjoyed—the day settling down peacefully instead of the creeping grip of night he half-remembered from life before his accident.

"What was that all about?" he said as he dried off a pot, keeping his tone light and casual.

"What?" Amelia plunged her hands into the sudsy sink.

"The Klondike wedding track record."

Her shoulders fell. "Oh, that." The sad tone confirmed Finn's theory that she was only talking about the wedding track record of one particular Klondike—her.

He suddenly felt bad about bringing up the subject. "Hey, you don't owe me any explanations."

She pushed out a breath, sending a little flurry of bubbles into the air. "It's no secret. Everybody knows."

"I don't. Tell me."

She ran a finger in small circles through the suds. "His name was Rafe Douglas. He was— still is—a Ranger down by San Antonio. We would have been married by now, but I broke off the engagement a month before our wedding."

The regret in her words was such a contrast with the optimistic Amelia Klondike he was coming to admire. "What happened?"

"Work always came first with Rafe. I thought

I knew that—the missed dinners, the constant phone calls, that sort of thing. He was on the fast track, dedicated, rising up through the ranks. People looked at him like he was a hero—the whole 'one riot, one Ranger' package—and he was." Finn felt his throat tighten. The phrase 'one riot, one Ranger' was an old Texas story about how it only took one Ranger to quell a whole riot—he knew that. But did everybody know that? The words buzzed at him with an unnamed importance that he stashed away to think about later.

Amelia dunked a saucepan into the suds as if she were drowning the memory. "I tried to feel proud of him rather than neglected. I did, mostly. But when he asked me if it would be okay to postpone the honeymoon for a big case that would earn his promotion, I wasn't as gracious as I should have been."

Gracious? The idea stabbed Finn in the gut. *What kind of man does that to his bride?*

Amelia began attacking the saucepan with a soapy sponge. "Gramps threw us an engagement party five weeks before the wedding, and Rafe was dreadfully late—so late he never showed. Some crisis on the force kept him in Austin." She stopped scrubbing, holding the pot up and watching the suds slide off it. Her eyes were on the saucepan, but her memory was at the party. After a pause, she passed the pot under the faucet, watching the suds slide off the shiny surface and swirl down the drain. "By the end of the party I realized the badge would always come before me, and my life would become one long wait for him to come home." She looked up at Finn as she handed him the rinsed pot, and her eyes were such wide blue pools of unhappy resignation that the sight pushed against his ribs. "Rafe was one of the last people to know I'd called off the wedding when he showed up four hours after the party ended."

Finn took the pot from her hands, lost for an adequate response. It explained the pity he had picked up on earlier. How anyone could cast Amelia Klondike off as a social charity case was beyond him. She was no old-timey spinster—she was still young and as vivid a beauty as he'd ever seen. An irrational part of him wanted to find this Rafe idiot and knock some sense into him, but he couldn't say where the strong emotion came from.

"It was all anyone could talk about for weeks." She flicked the soapsuds off her hands as if banishing the memory. "I became that cheerful cast-off everyone asks to lunch to be nice. I threw myself into helping other people because that seemed a better choice than crying over something I couldn't change."

"I'm sorry," he said, not knowing what else to say.

The faint echo of a smile turned up one side of her pink lips. "You and me both. I loved him. And he loved me…just…not quite enough."

Chapter Six

One riot, one man. It kept drumming through Finn's head while he tried to sleep. He heard the clock downstairs chime two in the morning—another Christmas carol, for crying out loud. He'd been staring at the ceiling for at least four different carols. Sleep hadn't come easy since his accident. When he did sleep, he often woke with the sense that his dreams were a tangled mess, even though he never remembered what they were. The continual unknowing and weariness was starting to get to him.

One riot, one man. Anyone even halfway familiar with Texas Ranger history could know that phrase, yet Finn had the sure impression that it was more to him. More what? And why?

His pulse began to do that pounding thing it did when he let the memory loss get to him. A baseless, focusless anxiety from which it was getting harder and harder to talk himself down. Doc Searle was right about one thing—it was bad to be alone when his situation swarmed around him like this. Finn sat up in bed and swung his legs over the side, putting his hand over his heart in a desperate attempt to will it calm. He felt the pounding beat under the cotton plaid of Amelia's gift pajamas.

It came to him right then. A sensation, rather than a visual, but clear and sharp as if someone had just pulled a curtain aside from a sunny window. He remembered the feel of his hand touching the metal circle of a badge. It came back to him in remarkable clarity—the engravings on the star, the way each point of the star met the metal circle around it, the feel of his shirt beneath the badge.

A Ranger badge. *His* Ranger badge. *I am a Ranger. Or at least I was*. The fact that he couldn't tell if he still was meant something— only he couldn't quite figure out what. If he wasn't, there was a big reason why he wasn't. He could feel the weight of the fact wrap around the memory like a blindfold, hiding any further information from his sight.

I am a Texas Ranger. It was the most certain thing he knew in days, as powerful as the sense that he disliked Christmas. The revelation shot him out of bed to pace the room, unsure of what to do with the new knowledge. *I am a Texas Ranger. I have that badge.* Finn stopped in the middle of the room, hands over his eyes, trying to pull a visual from the murk of his memory. He knew—somehow—that there was information on that badge if he could just see it. Finn squinted his eyes, nearly grunting with the effort, only to be rewarded with blank gray. Frustration knotted his gut and only the hour kept him from shouting, or throwing something, or anything to rage against this infuriating blank wall that always seemed to be at his back.

It's more than you knew before, he told himself, but it didn't help. He was a Ranger. Yes, that was useful. But now he was also wide-awake and steaming mad in the middle of the night.

He heard Bug's snorting little whuffs—that dog always sounded as if he had a head cold—and the faint jingle of the poor guy's ridiculous Christmas collar from the downstairs hallway. Poor Bug. The combination of his fat belly and his short legs imprisoned him on the first floor as sure as Luther's bad knees. Amelia was right; Finn had often gotten to the top of the stairs to find Bug staring up at him with what could only be described as a jealous longing in the pug's bulging eyes. Bug wasn't much in the way of company, but it was better than staying up here wondering what to do with himself. Maybe a snack would settle him enough to get some more sleep.

Finn opened his bedroom door and padded to the landing to find Bug with two feet planted on the bottom step, staring sadly up. Finn had the odd thought that maybe Bug could mount the steps when he was younger and leaner, and he remembered the victory of being at the top of the stairs. *Now you're turning everything into remembering and forgetting,* he chided himself as he made his way down the stairs to the grateful dog. He'd tried not to like the strange little beast, but Bug was always so happy to see him, the fat little guy had won him over.

Finn sat on the bottom stair and gave Bug a series of scratches. It made the Christmas collar jingle a bit, and Finn looked up to see Luther standing in the doorway to the kitchen. The fridge door was open, throwing a wedge of bluish light across the kitchen floor behind him. Luther had a brownie in one hand and his cane in the other.

"Howdy, sleepless," Luther said, holding up the brownie. "There's three more. Want to join me?"

Bug turned and waddled into the fridge, clearly thinking the invitation included him. "Absolutely." Finn exhaled as he rose, glad not to be alone with his storm of thoughts right now. Brownies sounded excellent.

Luther snapped on a small light from under one cabinet, casting the kitchen in a dim warm glow. He had a glass of lemonade out on the counter with another brownie on a napkin. "Grab a few for yourself and join me at the table." Luther narrowed his eyes and gave Finn a long look as he walked over to ease himself into a chair. "You look like someone just walloped you. Nightmare?"

Finn poured himself a glass, debating how much to share. He took two of the three brownies—despite feeling hungry enough to eat all of them—and sat down across from Luther. "Not exactly." He was grateful for the semidarkness; it made it easier to talk.

"You remembered something, didn't you?" Luther took a bite of brownie.

"How'd you know?"

"You're wide-awake and so annoyed you nearly twitch." Luther said. "Call it a good guess."

Finn didn't like feeling so transparent. Still, Luther was right—the discovery was humming inside him, needing to get out. Luther seemed as good a person as anyone—and certainly a better choice than Amelia given what she'd shared earlier this evening.

He elected to blurt it out. "I'm a Ranger. Or at least, I was. I think I still am, but it's all fuzzy."

Luther, thankfully, didn't seem fazed by the

news. "Well, that explains the police talk Amelia mentioned." He paused slightly, adjusting the napkin in front of him before adding, "I take it you know Amelia has a bit of…history…with them?"

"She told me about Rafe, yes." Finn ran his hands down his face. "I could know him, you know. We could be in the same company if I'm still on the force. Except, of course, I don't even know my own name."

"You're Finn."

"Sure, but is it my first name? Last name? Nickname? Nobody's reported a Finn missing."

"What does your gut tell you?"

Why was everyone always asking him that? "First name or nickname. It's what everyone calls me. I know that much."

"So things are coming back to you. Granted, not all you want, but some things, so I expect it's only a matter of time. I'll ask a favor of you, though."

"Sure. Anything I can do."

"Think hard about how and when you tell Amelia this. I know her—she'll go to Rafe if she thinks he can help. That wouldn't be such a good thing for her, if you know what I mean."

He hadn't thought about that. "Sure. I'll be careful about it. Maybe just hold off and see what comes back on its own. I can tell Dr. Searle at my next appointment and see if he can access force records."

"Amelia puts up a good show, but she's still hurting over what that man did to her." Finn saw such love for his granddaughter in Luther's eyes. The old man had every right to hold his place on the Rangers against Finn—and Amelia still might—but there was no judgment on Luther's face. Only regret and understanding. "It's a hard thing you're going through, son. You're in my prayers."

That felt good to hear. "Thank you."

"Are you a praying man, Finn?"

Finn shrugged. "I don't know. I don't think so."

"Might be a good time to start. Something this big happening to you? Seems to me God's up to something. When Amelia takes on a person as one of her projects—and you're one, if you haven't already figured that out—God's always up to something. She's got a sense. It's her gift, you know?" He broke off the corner of his brownie. "Ain't no stopping her once she gets it in her mind to help someone—I reckon you figured that out, too."

Finn actually felt himself smile. "I'm here, aren't I?"

"Yes, you are. Now eat up and let's try and get on back to bed. Tomorrow's comin' whether we like it or not."

* * *

Amelia watched Finn bang around the house Tuesday morning until his irritation and impatience were too much to ignore. She'd made him a hearty breakfast, and even let him do the dishes when he offered, but by lunch it was clear to the entire household that his day stretched too wide and empty before him.

He had just taken Bug for a walk—proof Finn was willing to occupy himself doing just about anything—when she stopped his pacing around the living room. "You're not used to sitting around doing nothing, that's clear enough to see."

Finn shrugged. "If I sit still I start thinking about everything I don't know."

Amelia knew that feeling too well. "I know what you mean. I'm the kind that needs to stay busy, too."

"Well, it's kind of hard when you don't know what it is your supposed to be doing."

This man needs a task, and quick. "Well," she said as brightly as she could, "maybe you just need to do whatever job's right in front of you. Why don't you come down to the church with me to the Here to Help office. I've got loads of stuff that needs doing for the upcoming Christmas party. And even more things that need putting away from the Thanksgiving event at the Lonestar League."

His eyebrows furrowed. "Are you the chairperson of *every* holiday in Little Horn?"

She laughed. "Well, now, I never quite thought about it that way, but I suppose it's true." She pointed at him, glad to see a hint of a smile on his features. "Don't you sell that brain of yours short, Finn—you're a clever one." She fished into her handbag and jiggled the car keys, which sent Bug to running frenzied circles at her feet. "Come on, Bug, let's go show off one of the best parts of Little Horn to our new friend." She'd wanted to get Finn inside Little Horn Community Church, and this seemed like the ideal way to introduce him to the little white church that was the heart of this small town.

Amelia often walked to her "office"—really a small room down the back hallway of the church basement—but she had several boxes of toys, clothes and food that needed to be delivered to the storage room. Finn was the perfect candidate to help her load the little trolley cart and take it downstairs, where Here to Help kept its resources.

"If you need something in Little Horn," Amelia said as she gestured around the room that was a food pantry, a lending closet, a store and a library all rolled into one, "it's my job to see that you get it. And if you've got something to give, it's my job get it to whoever needs it. After Daddy died,

I realized I had more money than I could ever spend in two lifetimes, so naturally I just started buying things for folks in need."

She touched a baby blanket on the shelf beside her as Bug settled down onto the bed he had in one corner.

"Most people I knew would just find more ways to spend money on themselves if they had your problem."

Amelia smiled. "Clearly, I am not 'most people.'" She loved her role facilitating folks' natural generosity.

"You buy all these things to give to people?" He sounded impressed.

"Of course not. I suppose I could, but it's much better that these come from lots of people. I just got things started. The good folk of Little Horn took it from there."

Amelia walked over to a shelf. "See these chemistry books? They came from Doc Grainger because Dora Peterson's boy couldn't afford the textbooks for his classes down at the community college." She patted the thick texts. "Now he'll be all ready to start after the holidays."

She moved one shelf over to hold up a San Antonio Spurs jersey. "Carson Thorn pulled a string or two to get this for Daniel Bunker's boy. He's going through chemo, poor soul, and this'll be waiting for him after his last treatment."

"That's amazing."

"Sometimes," she continued, "it's nothing so dramatic. Sometimes it's just an electric bill paid, or a bag of groceries at the end of the month, or a package of diapers and some formula." She looked at Finn. "I meant what I said when I told you Little Horn is a good place for you to be." She picked up a soup can from the the cart Finn had just wheeled in and placed it on the shelf with half a dozen others. "Sure, this little town can make me crazy some days, but I wouldn't dream of living anywhere else or doing anything else.

Finn picked up a can of black-eyed peas and did the same. "You run this all by yourself?"

"Of course not, silly." She picked up a box of spaghetti and put it next to several jars of sauce. "I have a whole committee helping me. And now I have you. Which is just perfect, because none of us can ever reach those top shelves where we keep the toothpaste." She handed him a tube and cast her eyes up to the higher shelves to illustrate her point. "Who needs a step stool when I've got a long, tall cowboy like you to lend a hand?"

Finn actually smiled. It didn't take a medical degree to see that his best treatment right now was to feel useful.

Amelia decided it was safe to take things a bit further. "If you master this, you'll get to help with the really fun part—Christmas shopping Friday night out at the mall by the highway."

Finn stilled, a can still in one hand. "What?"

She chose to ignore the look Finn gave her. "We have to shop out of town so nobody sees what they're getting for Christmas. Oh, I know you're not a big fan, but I need someone to help me lug all those toys home from the store. You'll help, won't you?"

"You want me to go to a toy store with you? *Christmas* toy shopping?"

Amelia plucked the can from his hands. "I see no one else lining up to make sure the children get their gifts at the League party. You're looking at Santa's chief helper, and I just deputized you into service."

"Amelia…"

"I promise it won't be more than four or five hours, tops. Four stores at the most. And when you see those children's faces…"

"Didn't you say you have a committee that works with you?"

She sat down on a crate—she was not going to let him give in on this. The man needed to be occupied and she needed the help. "And have to make six people keep secrets so that all the gifts stay a surprise? It was easier last year when Gramps could still push the cart, but Here to Help has always bought the kids' gifts and that's not going to stop just because I'm a little short of manpower. Not when I've got an able-bodied man with nothing else to do standing right front of me."

"I hate Christmas." His declaration grew more Scrooge-like every time he said it.

"I hate doing the paperwork, but it has to be done. It might actually be good for you. Maybe facing down whatever gave you all those bad memories will unlock some good ones. I remember every Christmas gift I ever got—surely you'll remember one or two as we go."

"A plaid scarf." The words seemed to fall out of his mouth, as if his irritation spilled it from somewhere in the back of his brain.

Amelia blinked. "What did you say?"

"I got a plaid scarf one Christmas. Ugly, scratchy thing that I hid in the garage and made up a story about losing it in the woods." Finn put his hand to his forehead as if struck by the memory. "Why do I remember some stupid detail like that? Why not something important?

Amelia put a hand on his arm. "Go on—what else do you remember?"

He shut his eyes, and she could watch him push past the block in his brain. "Red. I liked whoever gave it to me. Red," he said again, as if the repetition would command his brain to yield up more.

He pushed out a breath. "Nothing," he ground

out through clenched teeth with his eyes shut. "It's gone. Nothing."

"Hey," Amelia consoled. "It's not nothing. It's just not as much as you want."

"Not even close to as much as I want." He opened his eyes to look at her, impatience and frustration pulling his features tight. "Why can't I remember more?"

Amelia tightened her hand on his arm. "You will. Every little bit seems to unlock more. Isn't that how Dr. Searle said it would be?"

"I can't stand not knowing."

"Come with me on Friday. I need your help, and maybe that memory just now means all those presents might trigger more." When he shook his head, she tugged on his arm like an insistent child. "I need your help, and I think it would be good for you."

She stood there and waited until he threw his hands up in surrender. "Okay, you win. I'll go. But it's because you need the help, not because I think it will be good for me."

Chapter Seven

Amelia had never met anyone who didn't like Christmas shopping. She had been sure Finn would warm up to the idea as Friday night's gift hunt went on. After all, she was having loads of fun. "That red one, over there. And two of the blue ones." She pointed to a display of baseball hats in the sporting-goods section as she consulted her list. "Look at that, we're almost halfway done."

Finn looked at the cart, already piled gloriously high with toys, clothes and books. He ran his hand across the back of his neck. "Almost *halfway*?"

"With this store, yes." Maybe three stores had been too much. He was still recovering from an accident. Perhaps a stop in the store's little cafeteria might smooth things over. "Except, I need fries."

Finn looked around. "I think I saw the grocery items over there."

"No, silly, I mean I need to *eat* fries." She didn't, really, but Amelia knew suggesting *Finn, maybe you need to sit down and rest for a bit* would get her nowhere. "They make really good ones here."

"I suppose I could use a bite to eat and maybe a drink."

Amelia grabbed the handle of the cart and spun it resolutely in the direction of the snack area. "That settles it. We can finish the other half after I've recharged on grease and sugar."

He stared after her. "I've never met a woman who thinks the way you do about food." He caught up to her and took over cart pushing duties. "'Course, how would I know, right? It's not like I remember."

Finn had helped every day this week to stock the shelves at Here to Help, and it had definitely improved his spirits. Maybe he was finally making peace with his condition. He'd still put up a fair show of resistance over shopping tonight, saying he'd already done enough "community service," but most of that bluster had worn off in the first hour. He took pot shots at cheesy decorations, but he was genuinely helpful, just like he'd been in the church storeroom. He'd even made thoughtful suggestions for some of the boys.

Amelia was glad for his assistance—the cart was heavy and she'd have never made it this far without his help. "Oh, look, there are the DVDs— I'm supposed to get two John Wayne movies for Darren Taylor."

"There's a kid who likes John Wayne movies? Do kids these days even know who John Wayne is?"

"Everybody knows who John Wayne is. Even amnesia patients." A comfortable ease had developed between them over the past few days. She tried not to think about how much she enjoyed his company—there were too many unknowns. *Lord, couldn't I just get an eye for an uncomplicated man for once? Finn belongs to B—or at least he might. Help me guard my heart here.* She forced her focus back to the task at hand, scanning through the category dividers. "Westerns, please, not war movies."

It was wrong that she found Finn's exaggerated sigh so adorable, and Amelia bent her head over the movie selection even as she heard him flipping through the next rack over. She looked up when she heard him stop, only to see him staring at one, holding it up with an odd look on his face. It had a brash photo of John Wayne in a '70s suit pointing a gun. "Definitely not that one."

Finn didn't move. He just kept staring at the DVD. His breathing sped up and his knuckles went white from clutching the DVD so tightly. She stepped closer to him, alarmed. "Finn, what?"

"'Brannigan,'" Finn said, reading the title of the movie. "Brannigan."

"Brannigan what?"

He blinked and looked up at her. "That's my name. Finn Brannigan. My name is Frank Brannigan."

He looked a little unsteady, as if he would fall over if he didn't sit down, so Amelia stepped up close and held his shoulder. "Really?"

"Yeah," he said, his eyes wide. "I just know. Like it slipped back into my head just now. Frank Michael Brannigan. Finn's a nickname. I'm thirty-four years old." He grabbed her hand as it clasped his shoulder. "Amelia, I'm Finn Brannigan."

He was so desperately relieved that Amelia's throat turned to knots. "I'm very pleased to meet you, Finn Brannigan." His blue eyes were wide with wonder, as if the weight of the past days slid right off his shoulders with the memory. There was a little bit of fear in those eyes, too, and she understood why. Finn had never spoken it aloud, but she could tell he wasn't sure he liked the life he'd forgotten. While the fact he was Finn Brannigan opened dozens of important doors, not even Finn could say if good or bad news was behind them.

She *was* pleased to meet him. The man who wasn't yet Finn Brannigan had shown himself to be charming, earnest and steadily less sad. Would the return of his identity clarify that? Or could it tangle it further?

Finn looked around the store, gauging whether the world had shifted with his discovery. The rush of Christmas shoppers around them simply went about their hectic lives, oblivious to the huge moment that had just happened. "Wow," he said, one hand running nervously through his hair. He looked happy but lost, as if he didn't quite know what to do with the information he now had. Who would have words for finally remembering who you are?

"Maybe we really should sit down with those fries. Or cupcakes—this deserves a celebration of some kind and I saw some of those food trucks just down the street." He looked a little unsteady on his feet and Amelia wanted someplace more private than the movie section to help him deal with this new memory.

"Cupcakes or french fries?" His tone told her he found tiny cakes too dainty an option for a celebration. "Isn't there a third choice? Don't food trucks usually come in bunches around here?"

There were at least four trucks, but she'd only noticed the cupcake one. "It's a safe guess at least one of the ones back there offers barbecue."

She looked at the cart. It seemed wrong to keep shopping when such a momentous thing had just happened.

He gave her a boyishly excited look. "I'll buy you cupcakes, but I need some real food."

"Your credit card from the hospital is for basic living expenses, not celebrating." They'd bought him clothes earlier this week, including the green shirt he now wore. It set off his eyes in a way that flipped her stomach whenever she looked at him.

He grinned. She shouldn't have laughed at his exuberance, but his kid-on-Christmas-morning excitement made it impossible. "Food is a basic living expense."

"But, Finn…"

He held up a finger, energy practically sparking from his features. "No buts. I can't stand another minute of shopping. Not now." It was the most declarative she'd seen him, so she silently followed as he turned the cart toward the checkout lines.

He was Finn Brannigan now. He'd taken a huge step toward resuming his life, and that was a good thing. Wasn't it? As they stood in the checkout line, enduring a terribly ordinary task under highly unusual circumstances, a nervousness rose up between them.

She felt as if she had to ask. "Do you want to call Dr. Searle right now?"

He thought about it for a moment. "No. I don't want to page him on a Friday night. It can wait until morning—I'm not sure he can do much until then anyhow." It made Amelia wonder if Finn had come to the same conclusion: resuming his life would most likely pull him out of hers. *That's probably for the best*, she told herself. Finn's anonymity had created a bubble around their time together. He needed her, and his dependence—his companionship, really—struck a chord so deep she hadn't even realized it until just now when it might disappear.

He could change—he would have to change—once he knew who he was.

He was Finn Brannigan. The fact—at once fresh and familiar—hummed through his bones as he settled himself down on a picnic table beside a fire pit. The night air was pleasantly cool, crisp without being uncomfortable; perfect for a table near the roaring fire under the strings of Christmas lights that decorated the tables inside the circle of five food trucks. He was the closest thing to happy he'd been since this whole craziness started. It was a precarious kind of happy, a waiting-for-the-other-shoe-to-drop cheer, but he'd actually had fun tonight. He'd had fun doing something Christmassy, and the dark of the evening felt close and comfortable rather than eerie and lurking.

Amelia sat with three decadent cupcakes and a foam cup of hot chocolate. She'd been ridiculously gleeful about picking them out, grinning and thanking him as if he'd given her the moon instead of just a surefire sugar rush. He, on the other hand, had opted for a monster of a pulled-pork sandwich and a root beer. Evidently memory made him hungry.

"Was that fun?" Amelia asked. When the teenage girl behind the counter had asked him for a name for his order, he'd said "Brannigan" with so much enthusiasm that he earned a few stares.

"I guess it was. I don't think I'll ever take my name for granted again. The whole thing is so odd—I feel like everything's changed."

She peeled the bakery wrapper from the small mountain of frosting that passed for a cupcake. "Everything has changed, hasn't it?"

Finn heard the same catch in her tone that he felt in his own chest. He knew he was Finn Brannigan, but didn't know enough to deem that good news. The dark, heavy sense that the life he'd forgotten wasn't a happy one still pressed against him. After all, he was a Ranger—he must have seen his share of Texas's underbelly.

He hadn't yet told her. After Luther's warning

and the wounded way she talked about her ex-fiancé, he'd resisted.

"So it's just your name? That's all you remember?"

"And my age." *Tell her you're a Ranger*, the honorable side of him scolded the other part that foolishly refused to confess. It felt as if everything would slam back into place once tomorrow dawned, so would it be terrible to just keep this one night as the happy victory it was? She'd be perfectly entitled to refuse his friendship once all the facts came to light.

Despite the fact that he hadn't voiced any of those thoughts, Amelia picked up on his worry—this woman had more intuition than anyone he'd ever known. It was probably what made her so good at helping people. She laid her hand on his arm and he felt that surge of connection he had each time Amelia touched him. As if she needed him, even though he was acutely aware it was the other way around. The bonfire lit her eyes and cheeks with a cheery glow. "I can't imagine what you must be feeling right now."

She'd recognized the return of his memory was a double-edged sword. Would he ever be able to tell her what a gift her understanding was? "There's a lot floating out there—fuzzy impressions I can't quite get a fix on, but the name… I can't tell you what it means to know my whole name." He hesitated for a moment before admitting, "For a while there I was terrified it wouldn't come back. That I'd end up one of those freak stories you read about in checkout-counter tabloids."

She laughed. "I can't imagine you up there with the celebrity tragedies and alien babies. You're far too normal."

Normal? Nothing about him felt normal. The scary part was the constant sense that his normal wasn't anywhere near as nice as right now was, sitting out under the stars near a roaring fire hearing…

Christmas carols. A group of high school students had gathered in the corner of the picnic area and began to sing "Away in a Manger." Finn felt his stomach tighten.

"Oh," Amelia said, turning to look at the group, "this is my favorite."

Finn waited for the slam of pain that had almost made him ask her to take the kitchen clock down, waited for his unnamed aversion to all things Christmas to wash over him. It came, but more softly. More like regret than flat-out hate. Finn closed his eyes and tried to hear it the way Amelia did: reverent and quiet instead of slow and mournful. Why couldn't he grasp the big dark thing lurking just out of his reach? What made him react to Christmas the way he did?

He opened his eyes as everyone in the place

joined in the carol, a cozy little scene straight out of a TV holiday special. Amelia glanced back at him. "Do you remember the words?" she teased, half in jest, half in encouragement. She raised her voice with the others, a sweet, light soprano that wound its way around Finn's heart as he simply listened to the verse fill the dark sky.

Be near me, Lord Jesus, I ask thee to stay
Beside me forever and love me always
Bless all the dear children in thy tender care

From out of nowhere, that phrase cut through him with a bolt of grief he could neither stop nor explain.

And fit us for heaven to live with thee there

Something horrible and ugly roared up in his chest, clutching at his throat so that he had to gulp for breath. The sound drew Amelia's attention, her eyes growing wide at whatever horror showed on his face. "Finn?"

"Get me out of here," he gasped, fumbling to pull his long legs from under the picnic table.

"What?" She stood, worry replacing the joy he'd tried to bask in just seconds ago.

"That song. I can't..." *Can't stand it? Can't explain it?* No words would come, just a scraping sensation in his lungs that made it feel as if he was gulping down broken glass. It physically hurt, and it was more than just bruised ribs. He was dizzy again and nearly fell in his rush to exit the table. The stumble strained his side and made the pain that much worse. He'd have run if he could, anything to get away from the sweet voices singing that song.

He beat her to the car, falling against the side as if he'd run ten miles instead of the twenty-or-so feet it was. Even though he faced the car, he could feel the stares of everyone behind him, imagine their murmurs about the lout who made a scene right in the middle of the choir's charming performance. *You don't know what's happened to me!* he wanted to turn and yell—the exact opposite of the *I know my name* shout he'd given the counter clerk. *Even I don't know what's happened to me.*

"What's wrong?" Amelia caught up to him, grabbing at his shoulder.

"I don't know," he growled. How he loathed those three words. "The song. It hit me like a wall. That song means something bad to me. Something awful I just—" he rammed his fists up against his forehead as if he could knock the memory loose "—don't know."

She took his hands and pulled them down, holding them tight. "Finn, my heart is breaking. What happened to you that Christmas is such a horrible thing for you? What could be so awful?"

He started to say *I wish I knew,* but the truth was he didn't.

Chapter Eight

"It was heartbreaking," Amelia told Ruby Donovan as they sat in Amelia's kitchen Saturday morning. Amelia had brought over three dollhouse kits that were to be assembled for girls to receive at the League Christmas party. Finn had taken Bug for a walk, and Amelia took the opportunity to share this new worry with her friend. "His reaction was so awful and so strong—like it physically hurt him."

Ruby stirred her tea. "It sounds terrible. I can't imagine what it's like to go through something like that. Is he getting better?"

"I don't know. I don't think he knows, either. Doc Searle says he's progressing fine, but this hardly seems like fine to me." Amelia cupped her hands around the red-and-green mug. "They talked on the phone this morning when Finn told him his name, and Doc told him to come right over to the medical center Monday."

"That must feel like a million years from now if the doctor can tell him anything new. You said Searle is working with Lucy to dig through official records, right? Is there anything we can do to help?" Ruby asked. "He should come to service tomorrow. Carson would invite him to the church men's group if you think Finn would come."

"I actually think Carson and Finn would like each other, but church with all those Christmas carols and bible stories might be a bit much for now." Amelia saw the ring sparkling on Ruby's left hand and tamped down the little curl of envy that unwound in her stomach. Rafe had tried to make her keep the engagement ring he'd given her, but Amelia didn't want to have it anywhere near. "Have you and Carson set a date?"

"It's getting harder and harder for Iva to get around, so we'll need to make it sooner rather than later. I couldn't bear for her not to be there." Ruby's grandmother Iva was battling Parkinson's disease, and the past few months her symptoms had clearly worsened.

"Of course Iva has to be there. You'll let me know if there's anything you need for her, won't you?"

"You know I will. And speaking of weddings, did I really hear that Lizzie and Boone are going to have a circus wedding?"

Amelia leaned back. "So word's gotten out, has it?"

"Miss Winters was having breakfast at Maggie's Coffee Shop the other day."

The retired schoolteacher was the hub of Little Horn's gossip wheel. Amelia sighed. "I can only imagine what Miss Winters thought of that."

"No one has to imagine," Ruby commiserated. "She told us all plain and simple that Lizzie was crazy."

"I prefer the term *unusual* myself," Amelia chose to laugh rather than give in to the moan growing in the pit of her stomach. "Lizzie wants everyone to remember her wedding for a long time. Just think how elegant your wedding will look by comparison."

"Carson wants Brandon to serve as ring bearer. That tiny tornado couldn't be elegant if his life depended on it." Carson's five-year-old nephew, Brandon, was a bit of a handful.

"Weddings should be family affairs. And that boy is so cute he could fall flat on his face on his way up the aisle and everyone will still adore it."

"I sure hope so." Ruby nudged Amelia. "Hey, maybe everyone will feel the same way about Lizzie's circus."

"It'd be nice," Amelia mused, "but I'll just be happy if there are no elephants."

Ruby checked her watch and stood up. "If she

wants pony rides, tell her to give me a call. I've got lessons starting in an hour. Some of the girls want to groom Louie—is that okay? That horse is great with kids." Ruby ran a riding school as well as boarding horses, including Amelia's horse, Louie.

"Fine by me. Louie loves children."

Finn and Bug walked in the door just as Ruby was leaving. "Hi there, Finn," Ruby called amicably as the pair enter the house. "I see you've made a new friend."

"We have a mutual understanding," Finn said. Amelia was glad to see a smile on Finn's face when he said it.

"That means Finn takes him for walks and Bug lets him. Finn is of the impression that Bug is overweight."

Ruby leaned down and scratched Bug under the chin. "Of course you are, you tubby little thing. You're cute that way."

Finn shot Amelia a "see, I'm not the only one" look. Maybe Finn making friends in Little Horn was going to have some disadvantages.

Later that afternoon, Finn caught Bug staring at him as he sat at the kitchen table trying to assemble one of the dollhouse kits Ruby had dropped off. "I already took you for a walk," he said to the pug, who watched him with too much interest. "There's nothing to eat here."

"Be careful how you phrase that," Amelia said from her place beside him as she squinted at a tiny toy dresser. She was trying to glue together the furniture pieces as Finn handled the architecture. "Bug would gladly snack on several of these bitty pieces. That dog's definition of food is very broad."

Finn sat back in satisfaction after snapping the chimney in place. "How many of these do we have to do?"

Amelia cringed. "Three. I'm hoping the next two will be easier after we figure out how all these work." She was gluing tiny cushions onto a set of kitchen chairs. "They're darling, but they're an awful lot of work. And rather beyond Gramps's abilities—I sure am glad you're here or I'd be up all night."

"Feels good to problem solve, even if it's on a miniature level." Finn fit the second part of the roof in place. "Look okay?"

"Little Amy Callister will simply swoon when she sees it. She was very sick at Thanksgiving, and this looks just like that old house up on the hill where her parents lived when they first moved here."

Finn adjusted a loose shingle. "Did you grow up in Little Horn?"

Amelia got a faraway look in her eyes, the kind a person got when they reached back for a pleasant memory. It made him the tiniest bit jealous. "Mama and Daddy had a ranch just east of town. It was a wonderful place to grow up—all that space and sunshine. Daddy made some very smart investments after Mama died, but our early years were lean ones. Still, they were always full of love." She set the chair at its place next to the tiny table, her eyes sparkling with happy recollections. "Mama did Christmas like you wouldn't believe. Daddy used to say she went 'all out in a dozen directions.'" She looked up at him. "It's where I get my holiday spirit."

He found himself smiling as well, caught up for just a moment in her joy. "So Luther says." Then, to his surprise, he found himself asking, "Tell me a Christmas memory."

She raised an eyebrow. "It won't bother you?"

"Seems I need to borrow a few until I get back my own." It was an awkward thing to say, given the hunch that his holiday memories were far from bright, but part of him truly did want to borrow her joy for a moment.

"The year I got my dog Sparks was the best Christmas. Mama and Daddy hid that puppy in the barn until Christmas morning. After we'd opened our few presents, they made Lizzie and I so mad by telling us we still had chores to do even on a holiday. We were spitting mad as we walked to the barn until this brown fluff ball in a big red ribbon came bounding out with Mama and Daddy right behind." Amelia patted her lap, which sent Bug waddling over to her, tail wagging. "Next to you, Bug, Sparks was the best dog I ever had." She leaned down to pick up Bug and snuggled him in her lap. Bug rewarded her with a sloppy kiss followed by a sneaky attempt to snack on some of the doll furniture, a mission she thwarted with a hearty laugh and a gentle swat on Bug's nose. "Bug is marvelous company, and Sparks was, too. He was a big, gentle mutt as loyal as they come. Lizzie and I fought over who got to sleep with him when Mama died, even though we were in our teens."

Finn stopped assembling the house. "How did you lose your mama?"

"Pneumonia. I think it started out as some other infection but when the pneumonia set it, she just couldn't fight it off. First she was sick at home, then in the hospital, then in intensive care…" Her voice trailed off. He thought about how much he hated being in the hospital, how much nicer it was to be in a home—even someone else's—and sympathy made him want to touch her hand. He didn't.

"The first Christmas without Mama was the worst. I kept trying to make it big and wonderful in her place, for Lizzie and Daddy as much as for myself, but nothing worked. I couldn't do anything the way Mama did, but I didn't know what else to do."

Finn looked around the kitchen covered in holiday decor. He'd never seen anyone decorate *every single* room of their house in so much holiday cheer—except for his upstairs, thankfully. Even the bathroom had little trees and lights and special towels. "Seems to me you picked up her knack." He pointed for emphasis at Bug's Christmas sweater, a red-felt thing with little green trees all down the back. He'd counted five different holiday sweaters for the dog already.

"I did, eventually." Amelia scratched Bug under the chin and was rewarded with a hearty lick. "I found my own way rather than trying to duplicate Mama's. But her love, her joy? I try to imitate that every day."

"You do," Finn felt compelled to point out. "You've got more joy in one hour than most folks get in a month. A life, maybe." Here she'd had so many hard knocks—parents gone, heart broken and who knew what else—and she still bubbled with joy and spent her days making other people happy. Where did that kind of bottomless well of mercy come from?

Her cheeks went pink with the compliment, and she fiddled with a bit of fuzz on Bug's sweater.

"I mean it," he said. "You're amazing. That Rafe fellow was an idiot, if you ask me." Finn swallowed hard, thinking that remark went a bit too far. If no one cared enough about him to recognize him missing, he hardly qualified to pass judgment on Amelia's relationships.

Her eyes came back up to meet his. Finn kicked himself for bringing up Rafe when they were supposed to be talking about happy holiday memories.

"It would never have worked between Rafe and me. He just realized it before I did, that's all." There was so much regret in her words.

"But he couldn't work up the spine to tell you? Instead he just goes no-show on you at your own engagement party?" The words came out sharply; Finn really did want to slug this Rafe guy for stomping on Amelia's heart the way he did.

Amelia let Bug hop down off her lap and began arranging chairs around the tiny table. "He did tell me, in a hundred small ways. I just wouldn't see them." She capped the glue bottle. "I can be a mite single-minded, if you hadn't noticed."

He had noticed. He wouldn't be here if it weren't for that single-minded nature. "Thank you again," he said softly, "for rescuing me. I may have forgotten a lot of things, but I don't think I'll ever forget what you've done for me." Mushy words, to be sure, but he felt all of them. "I don't know where I'd be right now if it weren't for you."

She gazed at him for a long moment, and Finn felt his breath catch in his chest at the blue of her eyes. He felt the closest thing to safe he'd felt in days, despite the temporary nature of his whole world right now. Did she feel it, too? That pull between them that went far beyond rescuer and rescuee? It didn't make sense, but he couldn't help feeling she didn't just find him in the woods—somehow, they'd found each other.

Only, if he really was a Ranger, couldn't his job consume his life the way Rafe's had? It was easy to say no now, while none of that life invaded, but his old life would eventually return—maybe huge pieces of it when he met with Searle Monday—and who knew what would happen then?

He forced a light tone into his words as he picked up the door piece of the dollhouse and began working it into the side wall. "I doubt I'd be spending my Saturday nights playing toy maker, that's for sure." The door frame snapped into place. "Two more of these?"

From the corner of his eye, he watched Amelia fold the moment away, taking her "let's not go there" cue from his unspoken retreat. "Yes. But then we'll have to get started on the bicycles."

Chapter Nine

Finn was glad Dr. Searle had given him Monday's first appointment of the day. The weekend had dragged by, his impatience nearing the breaking point. Today would unlock everything. Details would start coming faster and faster until he had his whole life back.

He'd expected Searle to be as pleased with the breakthrough as he was, but the doctor's expression hit Finn as squarely as if the office door had slammed in his face. Searle didn't have good news. The prickly ball of anxiety in Finn's stomach solidified into a lead weight.

"Come on in, sit down."

Searle placed his hands on a single file sitting on his desk. Finn noted *Frank Brannigan* typed on the tab, but the rush of excitement was now one of fear.

"Did you keep your promise to stay off the internet?"

"Just about killed me, but yeah." Searle's request had made a bit of sense—he could indeed end up chasing rabbit trails of false information or wrong identities and he wasn't in strong enough emotional shape to handle big shocks—but given the doc's face, it hadn't saved Finn any grief.

Some part of Finn—the Ranger instinct, maybe—recognized the carefully neutral face Searle wore. One steeled to relay bad news. Finn gritted his teeth. "With your full name and the information you told me," Searle explained, "I was able to make contact with the Rangers and they sent over your confidential file. Did you happen to remember anything else other than what you've already told me?"

Finn recognized the stall and fought the urge to reach out and grab the file out of Searle's hands. "Just tell me, Doc. I can already see it's not happy news, so let's just get it over with, okay?" His heartbeat thundered under his ribs, making them hurt from the tension building in his whole body.

Searle took a deep breath and opened the file. "You are a member of the Rangers—Company F out of Waco, to be precise, but you have been away from Waco and on leave since February."

Leave? As in placed off duty for a reprimand? "What'd I do?" he gulped out. Based on Searle's face, it was something huge.

"Nothing you did, Finn. More what…happened to you."

"Happened to me? I'm here, aren't I? I've got no injuries other than the ones from when Amelia found me. What's in there?"

The doctor adjusted his glasses. "Not exactly to you." He took another deep breath. "But we know *B* stood for *Belinda*."

Stood. Finn felt the past tense of Searle's words wrap around his throat.

"Rangers as a rule shy away from any press, but you can see why they had extra cause to keep this quiet. You were with a special ops unit, Finn, and something went wrong. All the details are in there."

Finn scanned a gruesome photo of a car wreck and a few sentences of the accompanying report. Belinda's car had been sabotaged by associates of someone Finn had helped to put in jail. The room spun around Finn in angry circles, yanking him off balance and stealing the air so that he couldn't breathe. An excruciating combination of grief and numbness—after all, how could he grieve someone he didn't remember yet—came at him as if someone was hurling rocks at his chest. *Belinda.* He desperately wanted the name to mean something, to call up a face, a house, a life, anything, but nothing came. Finn wanted to get up and run somewhere, anywhere, but his limbs wouldn't obey. Instead, he felt as if he were melting on the spot, losing all the things that held him in place, threatening to disappear into thin air.

And hadn't he? He *had* disappeared. Who wouldn't want to disappear from what Searle just described? He looked back to the report and saw the terrible word *infant*. He'd had a baby? A baby daughter who had been lost, as well? Finn's whole body shook. For one horrific second he thought, *I wish I never knew,* only to feel even worse for wishing it. The unfocused pain, the sheer faceless tragedy of two lives needlessly lost, pressed down upon him until he thought he was going to black out.

"Finn?" Somewhere from beyond the swirling room Dr. Searle's voice was calling to him, and there was a hand on his arm but Finn felt he was a hundred miles away, somewhere black and painful. "Finn? Do you want me to call someone?"

The stinging truth of that question snapped Finn's eyes to the doctor's face. "Who? Who? There's no one to call, Doc. I'm alone. That's why no one's come looking for me. There is no one."

"The Rangers had no idea you were missing until our call. They're worried about you. They offered to send someone—a counselor trained in this sort of thing."

"No!" Finn didn't even need a second to think about it. "No. I'm alone in this." He finally made his hands move, willing them up to cover his eyes, where the cold, fluorescent overhead light hurt too much all of a sudden. At least the pain was something to feel, some human reaction he could hope to understand.

"I wish you'd reconsider. This is more shock than anyone should handle without…"

"Did they get him?"

"Who?"

"The guy who did this!" It came roaring out of Finn with a startling rage. He didn't bother to hold it back; it was something to feel, the only thing that made him human at the moment. Even a senseless anger was better than the hollow, horrified emptiness that threatened to swallow him right now.

"Yes. But he died of the gunshot wound inflicted when they brought him in."

"What was his name?" Finn began rifling through the pages of the file.

"Why do you…"

"Tell me his name, Doc!" Surely, Finn would never totally forget the name of the man who murdered his family. If anything would unleash the flood of recollection that even those images in the file could not unlock, it would be a man he surely hated above all else.

"Tony Stone. His name was Anthony Stone."

Finn waited for the awareness to break open,

for the anger to find a target so it could go out instead of pounding down upon him, but it didn't happen. It was as if he was looking in on someone else's life, hearing atrocities that happened to some other man. *It's me*, he kept reminding himself, *that's me. It happened to me. To my wife. To my child.* For a ridiculous moment, he understood why his brain had betrayed him so; what man on earth wouldn't forget all that pain if he could?

"I'm so sorry, Finn. I wanted better news for you. We all did."

"Who else knows?"

"What I've just told you?" Searle replied.

"Yeah, who else knows?"

"I wouldn't release this information to anyone without your consent, Finn. No one else knows except the Ranger headquarters in Austin. And like I said, they've offered to send someone over here and I think you should…"

"No," Finn shot back, throwing the file on Searle's desk. "I'm not ready for them. I'm technically on leave still, right? I don't have to talk to them?"

Searle picked the file up. "They're deeply concerned about you, Finn. You've been through a horrible ordeal, now made worse by your recent accident. There was a counselor assigned to your case back at the time of the accident. Let me call him. You need assistance getting through something like this."

"No, I don't. I don't need anything." Everyone knew more about him than he did. He'd forgotten so much, Belinda and—with a stab of torment he realized he didn't even know his own daughter's name—were just facts on a page. Facts that must have been his fault. The room began closing in on him again. "I don't want anyone from the Rangers here. I don't want *anyone* here." He glared at Searle. "No one else hears this. *No one.* I'll say something when I'm ready, when I remember them, but not one moment before, understand?"

"Finn, I don't think that's wise."

"Well, it's not your call, Doc, is it?" Finn shouted. Right now, he needed to be alone. Solitary, in some wide-open space big enough to handle the explosion of pain when it came. Because it would. It had to. He grabbed the file out of Searle's hands without asking whether or not he could have it, glad when Searle didn't resist. There was a park of sorts out back behind the medical center, and Finn knew he had to go there until he could get the rage and hollowness under control.

"Don't call Amelia. I need to be on my own. I was going to walk back when I was done anyways. You are to say nothing, not one bit of this to her." He pointed at the doctor. "Do I have your word?"

"Finn…"

"Do I?"

Searle was at least smart enough to know when negotiation was not an option. "There are a lot of people waiting to help you."

Finn stuffed the envelope in his jacket and headed for the door. "Well, they're all going to have to wait."

Lizzie's request to meet for breakfast comforted Amelia that things hadn't gone entirely south between her and her sister. She was more than glad to spend time with Lizzie at Maggie's while Finn was with Dr. Searle, even if her intuition told her the sisterly invitation meant something had gone wrong.

The coffee shop was crowded. Judd and Anne Derring were there, enjoying a breakfast with their foster children, Timmy and Maddy. Gareth and Winston McKay—Byron's teenage sons— were there as well, so it it must have been a "late start" day at school today. The McKay boys and half the shop were talking about the latest "Robin Hood gift," a set of bicycles for the Ramierez boys and some new equipment for their rancher father, who'd had a rough time of it since his wife left.

As they settled into their booth, Lizzie leaned in. "Fess up now, Lia, were those bikes from you?"

It was flattering—in an annoying sort of way—that people continued to suspect she was behind these gifts no matter how many times she denied it. "I don't give anonymously. I give because God's blessed me to bless others. I want them to know God's hand in all of this, so no, again, it's not me."

"Well, then—" Lizzie sat back "—who's been doing all of this?"

"I have no idea. I know Lucy has her theories."

"Which are?"

Amelia gave her sister a sharp look. "I wouldn't stay friends with the sheriff for long if I didn't know when to keep my mouth shut, would I?"

"Are they close to catching him?"

"I don't know."

"Is it someone from Little Horn?"

Amelia considered ordering pie for breakfast. "I don't know, Lizzie. Besides, we came here to talk about the wedding. What did Boone's parents say when you told them your plans?"

Liz looked down. "They weren't too keen on the idea, actually."

Amelia suspected that was an understatement. She'd met Boone's folks once, and they didn't

strike her as subtle. *I bet that stings. Show grace.*
"How so?"

"Well, Boone's dad said it was ridiculous."

Ouch. Then again, hadn't Gramps said something similar? At least he'd never put it quite so sharply to his granddaughter's face. "I'm sorry, Lizzie. You were so excited about the whole thing."

"Oh, they can say whatever they want. Boone and I are still going through with it. It's our wedding, after all."

A circus wedding was bad enough, but a *defiant* circus wedding? This looked like a marital nightmare on any number of levels. "And what does Boone say?"

"He's behind me one hundred percent. He told his father if he doesn't like the theme, he doesn't have to come."

Amelia could just imagine how that went over. "It's your wedding. You want his family there. His family will be part of your life together. You wouldn't dream of getting married without Gramps there, would you?"

Lizzie's eyes flashed. "Why? Does Gramps have a problem with what we want, too?"

"He wants you to be happy. I'll admit, he found the whole thing a bit—" she searched for a word that would keep the most peace "—unusual, but…"

"Why can't anyone see how much fun this will be?" The whine in Lizzie's voice sounded far younger than her twenty-four years.

"Maybe folks just think of weddings as more solemn affairs. It's a big, important step. A circus may sound a little more like a birthday party than two people committing their lives to each other."

Lizzie's eyes told Amelia that last remark had been a step too far. "So you don't like it, either."

"I'm not saying that. It's not mine to say in any case. But if you want my honest opinion, it might make everyone happier if you tone it down just a bit. We can still have lots of fun with the idea, just…"

"So you do hate it. How can you hate it? It was your idea. Boone said you were brilliant for coming up with it."

It was the first compliment Amelia could ever remember receiving from Boone. At least that was something. "I don't hate it." She recalled the sparkle in Lizzie's eyes that day that was clearly gone now. "I think maybe we might need to tweak it a little, that's all." The more prideful part of her worried Lizzie had told the world her brilliant big sister had come up with the idea. Just what Amelia needed—more Little Horn tongues wagging about her.

"Why don't you and Boone come for dinner tomorrow night. We can all talk about it then."

"Maybe." Amelia was glad Lizzie at least considered it. All too often, she dismissed a diner invitation right off, especially if Boone was involved. Boone never did seem to have much time for family—he was too much like Rafe in that way. "Is that amnesia guy still staying with you and Gramps?"

"Finn?" Amelia was glad to be able to give him a full name now. "His name is Finn Brannigan. Well, Frank Brannigan, technically—Finn's just a nickname. That much came back to him Friday night. He's with Dr. Searle talking about it right now."

Lizzie's eyes grew wide. "So who is he? It's like a grown-up version of baby Cody Stillwater. Finn wasn't some baby left on your doorstep, but still, it's a mystery right out of a movie."

Tiny Cody Stillwater had indeed been left on Grady Stillwater's doorstep with nothing more than a cryptic note, but Amelia didn't think the comparison made any sense. "No, it's not. It's a medical condition from his accident. One from which he expects to make a full recovery."

"Still, now that you know his name, you must be able to find out more, right?

"I think that's between Finn and Dr. Searle, Lizzie." The waitress set their menus down in front of them. "The man has a right to some privacy."

"He's staying in your house. Don't you want to

look him up on the internet or something? Don't you know anything else about him?"

Finn had groused loud and hard about Dr. Searle's request to hold off on internet searches, and Amelia didn't think it fair to go behind Finn's back and look herself. "I think Finn's identity should be Finn's business, not mine."

Lizzie ordered a ham-and-cheese omelette. "He's handsome, that's for sure. Great eyes. Tall, too. You like tall men."

Amelia ordered banana cream pie and raisin toast. "Yes, he's a very nice-looking man. And most likely taken, so stop that line of thinking right now. He was carrying a watch that said 'all my love, B.'"

"How mysterious and romantic."

You were once a smitten young woman who saw the whole world as romantic, Amelia reminded herself. She felt much older—and perhaps too much wiser—now. "I doubt Finn would share your opinion. It's torturing him that he cannot remember his wife or even if he has one."

"What do you mean, 'if'?" Lizzie cut her toast in neat triangles, the same way their mother had done. It always warmed Amelia's heart to know both she and her sister kept such details of Mama alive. "I thought you were sure he was hitched."

Hitched was Amelia's least favorite term for

the sacrament of marriage. "I think he is, yes, from the inscription and the way he talks."

"The way he talks?"

"A man who has loved sees the world differently. It's something in the eyes, in the way he describes the world." She looked at her sister. "Didn't Boone change when he fell in love with you?"

"Oh, yeah," Lizzie said with dreamy eyes.

Lizzie and Boone clearly loved each other. Only Amelia had learned that love wasn't always enough to make things work. It was the best start of all, but it was still only a start. Finn was a man who had loved. Amelia just wasn't yet sure he was a man who had loved and lost, or just loved and *been* lost. It was why she had to guard her heart so carefully here. "Maybe now that he's remembered his name, it won't be long before everything else comes back to him." She made herself add, "And he can go home to the life he has waiting for him."

They ate for a bit in silence, each woman sorting through her own thoughts, until Amelia's cell phone rang. "I'm sorry, Lizzie, I thought Finn was going to walk home when he was done," Amelia said as she fished through her handbag for the phone. "I'll just tell him it'll be a few minutes more."

Amelia was surprised to see Lucy's name come up on the phone screen. "Amelia?"

"Hi, Lucy."

"Where's Finn?"

Maybe Lucy had uncovered some new details. "With Dr. Searle."

"Are you sure?"

Amelia didn't like the sound of that. "That's where I dropped him off."

"Is he wearing that red plaid coat you gave Gramps last Christmas?"

She had to think for a minute before she realized Gramps had lent it to Finn because the coat he'd bought himself wasn't quite warm enough for the chilly day. "As a matter of fact, he is."

"Well, then, Finn isn't with Dr. Searle."

"What do you mean?"

"I just drove past McKay Park and Finn is sitting on the ground in the middle of it with his head in his hands."

"He's what? Did he fall? Does he look ill?"

"I can't say for sure. I think you'd better get over here."

Amelia pulled a $20 bill out and tossed it on the counter. "Something's wrong with Finn. I've got to go. I'll call you later about dinner, okay?" She raced out the door, her heart twisted tight in worry.

Chapter Ten

Amelia had never driven so fast through town. She swerved her SUV into the parking space beside Lucy's truck and felt her heart drop to her boots when she followed Lucy's silent point to a figure slouched in the middle of the park. Not even on a bench, just slumped on the ground as if the brown winter grass had reached up and yanked him down. If a man's pain could be seen by the set of his shoulders, this was a desperately unhappy man.

Lucy rolled down the truck window. "You want me to go with you?"

Dr. Searle had told Finn something upsetting—that was easy to see. Amelia knew enough of Finn's nature to know he didn't need a crowd around him now. He'd taken himself out here in the wide open for a reason, but even she knew his urge to be alone could be his worst enemy right now. Hadn't she taken him in just to prevent something like this? "I knew I should have gone to that appointment with him." She'd tried, but Finn had refused, and she had no right to impose no matter how many warning bells her intuition set off.

"Don't come with me, but don't leave. Just stay and pray, okay?" Amelia grabbed the wool blanket out of her backseat and began walking toward Finn. Normally so large, he looked small and beaten out there in the wide-open lawn of McKay Park. *Lord*, she prayed as her boots crunched across the winter grass, *he looks like a time bomb about to go off. Help me help him.*

He didn't notice her approach—something out of character for him; Finn was always keenly aware of his surroundings. Keeping some distance, Amelia circled around until she stood in front of him. "Finn," she said as softly as she could given the twenty or so feet between them. "What's wrong?"

He looked up at her with eyes that were ice-cold. She'd seen anger, frustration and even annoyance in his eyes before, but the frigid distance she saw now sent a chill skittering down her spine. "Nothing." His clipped, empty tone didn't even bother trying to gloss over the denial of that statement.

Amelia spread the blanket out between them

in an invitation to come off the cold damp grass, but he ignored it. She sat down on the corner farthest from him. "Something is definitely wrong."

He neither replied nor met her gaze.

"You don't have to tell me what it is. Come home and sort it out on your own there, not in the middle of the park like this." The pain was radiating off him, making the air feel twice as cold as it already was.

"So Searle called you even though I told him not to. Nice to know the amnesiac's wishes don't count for much." He gave the medical term an edge of disgust.

"Dr. Searle wouldn't go against your wishes. Lucy called me. She saw you sitting in the middle of the park and was worried."

That made him look up at her. "Worried I'd gone off my rocker?"

"Worried you were ill or hurt." After a moment, she added softly, "Why is it so hard for you to get that people here care about what happens to you?"

He shook his head. "I'm just some guy you found in the woods." He didn't say the word *worthless*, but it colored his tone nonetheless.

"Finn Brannigan, if you don't know that you're more than that, then more than your memory is messed up." She hadn't meant to say that much. This was hardly the time to admit what she was coming to feel for him, but his eyes did that to her—pulled things out of her she wasn't ready to reveal. She had an urge to touch him, to give him any kind of solace she could, but she could see that wouldn't be welcome. "Why did you come out here?" It seemed like the only safe question to ask.

"I needed space. I needed to be alone."

"Did Dr. Searle tell you something?" That seemed obvious, but it might at least uncover some hint as to what had hit him so hard.

He didn't answer, and the way his spine stiffened, she half expected Finn to get up and walk away.

"I've no business prying—I get that. But I've never seen you so upset and I want to help. I can't imagine what you're going through."

"That's right," he shot back. "You can't."

Amelia didn't have a reply for that. What was there to say to a situation as drastic as Finn's? "Can you tell me anything? Anything at all?"

He didn't reply, and Amelia decided to wait him out. She pulled the blanket up around her, determined to stay until he opened up or sent her away. He was at a dangerous crossroads— anyone could see that—and she would not leave him alone.

It seemed like half an hour before he looked up at her. At least this time his eyes were storm clouds rather than daggers. "Do you remember when I said I don't think I was a happy man?"

"Yes."

"Now I know why. Only it's worse than that. I know, but I don't remember."

Amelia wasn't quite sure what that meant. "I'm not sure I understand."

"Dr. Searle found some facts about me. Some awful things, really. But it's like they happened to someone else. I can't remember the people or what happened."

"You will, just not yet. Your name came back, didn't it?"

Finn sunk his forehead into his hand. "That's just it…it's coming after me, the memory. I should remember it, I need to remember it, it'd be wrong to forget it…only it'll be ten times worse than it already is when I do."

He rubbed his head as if the lack of memory hurt, and his anguish jabbed under Amelia's ribs. He wasn't making total sense, and he looked as if he'd topple over any second from sheer exhaustion.

"Why don't you just tell me what Dr. Searle said? Maybe I can help."

"No." The word was sharp and determined.

"It can't be as bad as your thinking, Finn."

"Oh, there's where you're wrong. It's worse. And it will only get worse from here. You should have just kept right on walking in those woods, Amelia. I'm no rescue for the likes of you."

Now he was scaring her. "Don't talk like that. Everyone's worth rescuing. You've just hit a bad patch, that's all."

The moment she spoke the platitude, Finn shot her such a hopeless, angry glare that she regretted it. No one should call whatever torment was pressing down on Finn "a bad patch." It was terrible and massive, and Amelia didn't know what to do. She only knew leaving Finn to his solitude would not only be cruel, but downright dangerous. Honestly, he looked like a man who would do anything, save for the exhaustion she could see pulling him down.

"Please, Finn, come home. We'll find a way through it."

He looked off toward the edge of the park, but his unfocused eyes told Amelia he wasn't really seeing anything except the black cloud he was so sure was hunting him down. "I'm so tired."

"So come home and rest. You've been through too much to do anything else, and you can't sit here in the middle of the park forever. You don't have to tell me a thing until you're ready, however long that takes." Amelia hadn't realized it until just this moment when she stretched out her hand, but she meant exactly that. Some part of her had become bonded to Finn and his journey back to himself. She had to see this thing through, even though she suspected it might cost her a large piece of her heart.

She kept her hand outstretched until, very slowly, Finn took it. "It's bad," he warned her.

She said the only thing she could. "I know."

Finn tried to remember. He locked himself in his room the entire day, going over every inch of the file. He stared at the photos of the mangled car, he read the horrible account of what had happened to his wife and child, he tried everything he could think of to bring their faces out of the black void. Nothing worked. The effort only made him dizzy, angry and sick to his stomach.

Finn glared up at the bedroom ceiling, up at the God Amelia claimed sent her to find him in the woods, and scowled in defiance. *This is cruel. I'd rather be dead than keep on this way.*

That seemed a dangerous statement to make to God, but Finn figured if He really did know everything the way everyone claimed, then his own black heart was no surprise to the Almighty. *So what are You gonna do about it?*

That really is my own question, isn't it? Finn had no idea what to do about the past he'd just discovered. Obviously, he hadn't handled it well before the accident—only, who could handle anything like that well at all? Sheriff Benson was investigating his accident site, but no one yet knew who had knocked him out. Were they still out there? If Finn gave in to his natural instincts to go crawl under a rock somewhere and hide, would his attacker come back and finish the job? Would he end up knocked out on some other ridge with no sweet, compassionately pushy Amelia to save him?

An hour ago she'd set a sandwich and lemonade outside his door and knocked gently. When he heard her go back downstairs, he retrieved the food but found he had no appetite. He was too stuffed full of emptiness to eat.

The hard, heartless truth was that right now there was nowhere to go. Searle had him file for the paperwork to replace his driver's license, but that wouldn't come until tomorrow. He could just get up and walk out of town, but that seemed pointless. He was still dizzy now and then, and a part of him worried he hadn't quite healed—at least in the medical sense. There was no hope of him healing in any other sense.

For the next twenty-four hours, Finn was stuck. Exhausted, miserable and stuck. So stuck he pondered going downstairs to fetch Bug so he could just sit here and listen to the dog snore beside him. He couldn't face Amelia and Luther, though, and Bug couldn't manage the stairs.

The dog couldn't get up, he wouldn't go down.

We're both stuck, buddy. Finn rolled over on the bed and quietly asked God to make him sleep for a week. Tomorrow seemed too near and way too hard.

here, it almost brushed Finn's mind even as the
bed on Tuesday, it's hard to tell. Cord to tell. first sleep
for a while. Finn's get seemed unmoved, and was
too loud.

Chapter Eleven

Worries over Finn stole Amelia's sleep, making it hard to paste a smile on her face when she saw Byron McKay through her front door window early Tuesday morning. He'd pressed the bell three times and was pacing her front steps by the time she got the latch open to greet his scowl. Thankfully, his persistence hadn't woken Finn—she wasn't ready to face Finn and Byron at the same time.

"Good morning, Byron."

"It's not," he growled. Gracious, didn't that man ever smile?

"I'm sorry to hear that. Won't you come in? Coffee's on." She'd made this morning's pot doubly strong in hopes of getting herself in gear, but even that and an extra-large serving of apple cobbler hadn't done the trick. Gramps hobbled in from the den and then wisely turned right around when he saw Byron. If only she could do the same. "What can I do for you?"

"You could do your job, Amelia. That'd be a fine start."

Amelia would liked to have said, *But I don't work for you*, but she knew better than to quibble about League volunteer loyalties with the likes of Byron McKay. The League was important to everyone, but it was absolutely the center of Byron's life—as much as anything but Byron could be the center of his life. "What's wrong?"

"The final timeline for the holiday party was supposed to be on my desk yesterday afternoon. It's not."

As if any party truly needed a minute-by-minute timeline. Byron expected everyone in the League to RSVP on time, arrive on time, dine on time and probably even leave on time. It had become the hardest part of planning League events, even the supposedly casual ones. The Christmas party was supposed to be all about the children's happiness, not timetables.

"I had something come up yesterday and I didn't get it finished. I've got a draft that we can look at together." She poured more coffee into her cup and set a second cup down in front of her guest. "Honestly, Byron, you've changed every timeline I've ever given you—I don't know why you don't just set it all yourself." Fatigue made that come out a bit harsher than was wise, so she amended, "That way you can have it exactly the way you want it from the start."

"The League Christmas party is a team effort. Everyone has to do their part for it to work."

Amelia grabbed her League file and sat down. Byron was always extolling the virtues of "team effort." Only trouble was, Byron's concept of a "team" was a lot of people obeying his commands. "I'm sorry I didn't meet your deadline. It was a bit of an emergency and quite unexpected." She slid the half-done listing of activities over to Byron's side of the table.

Byron shook his head as he scanned the paper. "Why are you always wasting your time getting tangled up in other people's problems?"

Byron, his wife, Eleanor, and their boys sat in the pews at Little Horn Community Church every Sunday. How could a man visit God's house every week and still not understand the virtues of charity and compassion? No matter how many times she explained the concept of Here to Help and its mission to Byron, he could never fathom why Amelia would spend so much time helping "folks who got themselves into fixes and ought to get their own selves out."

"I don't see it as a waste of time. I see it as the *best* use of my time. And we still have four days until the party—that's more than enough time to settle the agenda. Besides, it's the children's gifts that really matter here, not who gives what speech when."

"And are we on schedule with those gifts? Or have your emergencies derailed you on that, as well?"

Amelia took a long sip of coffee and mentally counted to five. "We're right on schedule, Byron. Finn's been helping me, so everything is going very well."

"Oh, him. Another one of your charity projects. Honestly Amelia, now you're taking in strays?"

"Maybe you ought to leave now." Finn's voice came dark and sharp from the kitchen doorway. "I don't know who you are, but clearly your manners didn't follow you into the house, so maybe you ought to head back out and find them."

Byron puffed up like an angry bull. No one ever talked to him like that—although Amelia could envision half the town of Little Horn standing behind Finn and applauding if they'd heard. "And you are…?"

Amelia wondered if Byron was truly mean enough to ask an amnesiac patient to state their name—or was Little Horn's gossip mill fast enough that everyone knew Finn had regained his identity? She hoped, for Finn's sake, that it wasn't fast enough to speculate on whatever had broken him down in the middle of the park yesterday.

Finn looked as if he'd slept no better than she had. "Finn Brannigan. The *stray* Amelia was kind enough to take in, to use your choice of words."

"Finn—" Amelia felt obligated to at least attempt a truce "—this is Byron McKay, vice president of the League we've been shopping for."

"The Lone Star Cowboy League you *generously volunteer* your time for?" Finn looked right at Byron when he said *generously volunteer*.

No matter how gratifying it was to have Finn say what she'd long been thinking, Amelia was in no shape to referee the fight brewing between these two men. "Well, Byron's a busy man, what with owning the largest ranch in town and all. He runs a tight ship," she offered, pasting a "don't start" smile on her face as she gathered up a copy of the activities list to hand to Byron.

"A ranch that was robbed again just last night."

That explained Byron's current bad temper. "What now?"

"Two pieces of very pricey equipment. Not even a year old, either of them. All those fancy security cameras didn't do me one lick of good with whatever low-life is thieving from this town. What it's going to take to get Lucy in gear to catch these hoodlums? I don't aim to wait much longer for action."

That caught Finn's attention. "You've got surveillance footage?"

"For all the good it does me. Half the ranches in Little Horn have installed cameras and systems to try and catch this crook, but things keep disappearing anyways."

Amelia was grateful the Finn-Byron standoff had been diverted for now. "And appearing," she offered. "Like I said, items go missing for some ranchers, while gifts appear for others."

"Yes. Items go missing from the prosperous ranchers, while handouts show up for the ones who can't keep their businesses afloat."

Byron grated on her nerves when he made such baseless judgments. "You know very well some of those folks face hardships that aren't their doing. Ben Moore's back injury—not laziness—has made times hard for the Moores." She handed Byron his files. "Those two little boys would be going without any Christmas presents at all if it weren't for the League and whoever is leaving those gifts."

Byron gave a snort even Bug would admire, but at least he didn't start up an argument again.

Finn, however, didn't want to leave it at that. "You should be grateful for folks like Amelia. Seems to me she's the best thing that ever happened to Little Horn. Sure am glad it's her who found me and not someone like you."

"Who do you think you are, talking to me like that?" Byron rose from the table, his beefy neck going red above the collar.

"I don't know—I'll tell you when it all comes back to me!" Finn snapped back.

"What's going on out there?" Gramps called from the den. She could hear him struggling to get out of the recliner at the raised voices.

Amelia pushed in between the men. "That's quite enough, you two. I've got plenty to handle without you two bulls locking horns in my kitchen." She took Byron by the elbow and led him toward the door. "Call me if you have any questions, Byron, and I'll let you know when all the gifts are bought. Finn, there's coffee in the pot and some cobbler in the fridge." Amelia had Byron out the door as fast as possible, leaning up against it when it shut.

"That man…" Gramps grumbled as he came down the hallway.

"Don't you start, too," Amelia chided. "You're limping again."

"I'm eighty-nine years old," Gramps replied. "Everything hurts. It's only a matter of which parts on which days." He brushed her concern off, but he was leaning much more heavily on his cane than he was yesterday. "Besides, I'm thirsty, and I wasn't sure it was safe to come in the kitchen before now."

Amelia checked her watch. "It's almost nine. I'll bring you some juice and your pills in a minute.

Gramps pouted. "I was hoping for more coffee."

"I made the coffee extra strong this morning. A second cup would have your belly aching in less than an hour."

"Fine." He waved his hand in surrender as he turned back toward the den. "Grapefruit, then."

Amelia let her head fall back against the door. "I didn't make it to the store yesterday, so I've only got orange."

Now it was Grandpa's turn to snort. Amelia looked at her grandfather's back, at Bug's indignant face at her feet and toward the kitchen, where Finn was probably snorting, as well.

I'm outnumbered, she thought. *Where's that Christmas cheer when you need it?*

Finn didn't know how to act around Amelia after yesterday. He'd stayed up in his room long after waking, both out of fatigue and sheer avoidance. He was being such a lout to her and yet she gave him nothing but compassion in return. The constant sense of feeling in her debt, feeling all the different things he was coming to feel about this woman, was tangling him in knots. And he was already in enough knots as it was.

Then that blowhard Byron started laying into her for not having some silly list done when she'd been in the park trying to put him back together. Even his awkwardness wouldn't let him stay upstairs while she took a beating for that.

He stared into the black of his coffee, feeling just as dark. Amelia wanted an explanation, and deserved one, but he wasn't ready. He couldn't bring himself to talk about Belinda until he remembered her, until she was more than a gruesome fact on a sheet of paper. He sheepishly busied himself digging through the fridge for toast or anything normal people ate for breakfast—not apple cobbler—as he heard her steps coming into the kitchen.

"Thank you," she said softly, forcing Finn to look at her even though he didn't want to. She had this fuzzy, snowy sweater on this morning that made her look like a fluffy cloud, all soft and airy. She always dressed in cheerful colors, and Finn wondered if he was the only person who could see that it did not entirely hide the dark he sometimes glimpsed in her eyes.

"For what?" As if he didn't know.

"For saying what I've wanted to say to Byron McKay for three years."

He handed her the orange juice from its place in the fridge door. "Why do you let that blowhard push you around like that?"

"Byron pushes everyone around like that. I learned long ago not to take it personally."

Finn shut the fridge door. "All the more reason for someone to put him in his place. You give to the League out of generosity. You help lots of people. You shouldn't have to cater to his ego."

"I'll admit he tries my patience sometimes. Lots of times. I just wasn't up to his bullying this morning." She reached for the pill sorter that held Luther's medications and poured a glass of juice for the old man. She took such tender care of her grandfather. Amelia took care of everyone, it seemed. It galled him that no one seemed to take care of her.

As if to prove his point, she brushed her weary expression aside and asked, "How are you?"

How was he? Barely holding it together. Confused, in too much pain, in not enough pain—there wasn't a simple answer to her question. "I'll live," he said.

"I know whatever happened yesterday was very hard on you. I'm sorry for that."

"Thanks." That was a lousy reply. He was deliberately withholding from her, and she was being so nice about it. He would have liked it better if she'd gotten steamed at him—it wouldn't add to the mountain of guilt that currently buried him.

He gulped down the coffee as she left with

Luther's medicine, grateful for the hot, strong brew and a moment to gather himself. He'd managed to read through the whole file last night, the terrible facts of his wife Belinda's and infant daughter Annie's death—no, Belinda and Annie's *murder*—and it had made him physically ill. Tony Stone had watched the Rangers bring down his entire counterfeiting ring and was near capture himself, with Finn leading the pursuit as part of a Ranger special operations unit. Just as they were closing in on arresting Stone he disappeared, and twenty-four hours later Belinda and Annie Brannigan had been found at the bottom of a ditch with their brake lines cut. They'd been Christmas shopping—a particularly heartless photo showed a trunkful of toys and gifts scattered across the crash site.

The only shred of good news was that the Rangers had managed to keep the incident out of the press so that Stone and his ring wouldn't be perceived as having scored a brutal victory. Stone had been killed by gunfire during the apprehension. He was dead before he could even be charged with the double homicide—the only thing stopping Finn from leaving right now to hunt the vile man down.

Very hard on him? Yes, yesterday was beyond unbearable. The only thing that would make it better—and infinitely worse—was for his memory to return. Belinda and Annie deserved to be remembered. He deserved to feel their loss a dozen times more than the empty hole he carried around this morning. A Ranger protected his own, and he hadn't done that, had he?

"I really am grateful for you what you said to Byron," she said as she came back into the kitchen. "So I'm going to give you a chance to bow out of tonight if you don't feel up to it."

"Tonight?"

"Oh, that's right, we never did get around to talking about tonight with all that…happened yesterday."

"What's tonight?" If she was going to make him go Christmas shopping again, he didn't think he could stomach the sight of wrapped gifts right now. The car-wreck photo was still burned so sharply in his brain that the toast tasted like cardboard.

"Lizzie and Boone are coming over for dinner tonight to discuss wedding plans."

"Hoping to talk her out of the three-ring circus?"

She laughed softly. "I am hoping to get her to tone things down, yes. But mostly I want to get to know Boone better."

Her narrowed eyes gave her doubts away. "You're not too keen on this guy, are you?"

"I wish I knew more about him. I wish he were

more eager to know us. He seems good at avoiding family gatherings." She sat back down at the kitchen table before looking up at Finn. "Lizzie and I only have each other. Gramps won't be with us forever. It's selfish, I know, but I can't stand the thought of her being pulled away from me."

The fear of being alone in the world was something Finn knew all too well lately. "Maybe she's just all caught up in the wedding stuff now. Once that calms down, you'll probably see them for Sunday supper every week." He couldn't say if any of that were true, of course, but Finn thought he ought to attempt some of the comfort she was always trying to give him. "I'll be fine for dinner. Just don't ask me for circus detail help, okay?"

That got a genuine laugh from her. "You've got a deal." She looked down at Bug, who was trying to angle himself up enough to beg a piece of toast from Finn. "Stop that, Bug. No begging at the table."

Bug sent up a whimpered protest. Sparked by an idea, Finn broke off a piece of the toast and stood up. "You want this? You're gonna have to work for it. Come here, boy."

He walked over to the stairs and made a big show of placing the bit of bread on the second step. "I know you want this. You know you want this. It's one step. Come on, Bug, show me what you're made of."

Amelia came to stand behind him, coffee cup in hand. "You're kidding."

"I'm tired of that dog making sad eyes at me from the bottom of the stairs."

"So you bribe the fat dog with bread and jam?"

Finn pointed at her. "Ha! So you admit he's fat."

Bug looked back and forth between Finn and Amelia, clearly aware the humans were ganging up on him. He put one paw on the first step.

"There you go," Finn encouraged. "Smell that bread and those raspberries. It's waiting for you. Get that other paw up there."

Bug sniffed toward the corner of toast, sat back on his haunches and then lobbed his round body forward to plant both paws on the carpeting of the first step.

Amelia cheered. Finn felt the first smile in what seemed like years cross his lips. The ensuing antics as Bug tried to get his roly-poly belly up over the edge of the stair sent Finn into outright laughter. Over and over the poor dog strove to get his body far enough up the first stair to reach the bit of toast until, at last and with a frantic scramble of back legs, he reached his goal. Finn cheered and patted Bug on the head as the dog squatted, panting and licking raspberry jam off his pudgy black nose.

"Well done, Bug," Finn praised, then looked up the flight of stairs. "Only fourteen more to go."

Chapter Twelve

After lunch, Amelia watched from the doorway as Finn and Gramps worked on assembling a toy tractor the model shop had sent over. Finn had still avoided talking about yesterday, but the hilarity with Bug had at least taken the sharp edges off his mood.

Gramps was another story—he seemed sour, bored and in more pain than usual today. She'd given him the model to occupy his time—he knew he couldn't help nearly as much with the Christmas gifts this year and it made him sad. *Age can be a cruel lesson in humility,* she thought. *Thank You, Lord, that Gramps is still sharp and still with me.*

She was also thankful how the two men were becoming fast friends. Still, what would happen to that friendship when Finn returned to his former life? Finn had managed to slide into a place in her life—and Gramps's—that had been empty for a long time. *Ah, but B may be mourning the empty space where Finn should be*, she reminded herself as the tug in her heart toward this man started up again. *Where are you, B? Why haven't you come looking for this amazing man?*

"That wheel goes there, doesn't it?" Finn had a way of helping Gramps without making Gramps feel helpless. She was grateful for that—too often people talked down to Gramps even though he still was smart as a whip.

"It does. That'll do it." Gramps chuckled. "We got it together, didn't we? I used to do models like these all the time when I was a boy." He narrowed his eyes at Finn. "You got the knack for it—I reckon you did, too." As he slid the newly assembled tractor into its box, he gave Finn a long stare. "Have you told her?"

Amelia eased back from the doorway. *Tell me what?*

Finn ran his hand down his face the way he did when he was troubled. "Not yet. I'm planning to today."

"You go gentle, like I said. She's had too much pain in that department, and I don't know how she'll take it. Rafe gave her good reason to think all Rangers make bad company."

"They're—we're—not all bad. I mean, I can't tell you for sure, but I don't think I'm the kind of person who would fall in with someone like Rafe. But it can cost a man a whole lot to be a Ranger, I know that."

Amelia leaned back against the hallway wall. *He's a Ranger.* She brought her own hands up to her forehead, at a loss for how to process the fact. *Finn knows he's a Ranger. And he hasn't told me.* That couldn't be all he knew now, not with whatever had made him so upset at the park yesterday. She hated the thought of Finn keeping things from her, but did she have any right to ask such disclosure from him? They had no real history together.

He has no history at all, she argued with herself. *How can I judge anyone for how they act under that kind of strain?*

"She's amazing, your granddaughter." Finn's compliment caught Amelia up short. "I've never met anyone like her. To have so many blows in your life and keep the attitude she has? I don't know how she does it."

"Amelia's faith is rock solid, son. That's how she does it. My son and her mama may have left her too soon, but they taught her that God is always, always watching over her. That's how she keeps the joy. You could learn a thing or two from her, if you don't mind my saying so."

Amelia had been thinking the same thing since watching Finn's pain yesterday afternoon. *He needs You, Lord.* How very like Gramps to come right out and say what she'd been holding back.

"I don't have that kind of faith." The emptiness in Finn's tone broke her heart.

"Well, do you have any faith at all? Do you know God is there?"

Amelia closed her eyes. *Say yes. Please let him say yes.*

"I do. But not in the way you and Amelia do."

She heard Gramps sit back in his chair. "Well, then, that's not hard to solve. Ask Him for it."

"Ask God for faith? Isn't that our department?"

Gramps laughed softly. "You got it all backward, son. Faith is given to us. We don't scrounge it up for God, you don't assemble it like this here model. It's His gift to us. It's there for the asking. But you're the one who has to do the asking."

Finn didn't reply. Amelia fought the urge to turn and look, to catch a glimpse of this astounding conversation, but she could not bear to intrude. She shouldn't even be listening in, but she couldn't have moved from the hallway for all the world.

"Can I give you a bit of advice, Finn?"

"Sure."

"Seems to me, now would be a mighty fine time to start asking. You've had something huge happen to you. God can use that, probably already has. Amelia says she doesn't think it's an accident that she found you, and I agree. God's got something up His sleeve, and I sure would hate for you to miss it."

It was a moment before Finn said, "Maybe you're right, Luther."

Gramps laughed again. "'Course I am. I'm always right. But don't you tell Amelia. I like to let her think she's right now and again just to be nice."

The laughter both men shared filled Amelia's chest until she could scarcely breathe. Gramps liked Finn a great deal. Even Bug liked Finn. But what to do about the fact that she was coming to care for him? *I don't want it to end, Father. He's a Ranger—and You know I wish that weren't so— but still I don't want it to end.*

Amelia checked her watch. It was two o'clock. She was going to have to break into this little scene soon if she and Finn were to get the deliveries done in time to get back and get dinner for Lizzie and Boone started. Maybe that time in the car, doing all the deliveries, would give Finn a chance to tell her directly about his being a Ranger. It mattered that he choose to tell her rather than overhearing it the way she had just done. Maybe he would finally tell her whatever was tormenting him so. Surely she could convince him keeping it bottled up was only going to make it worse.

Then again, she was just as guilty of not telling him what she was feeling, wasn't she?

Amelia counted to five, put a cheerful look on her face and popped casually into the room. "I don't know what you boys are laughing about, but I need Finn's help to go stocking right now if you can spare him, Gramps."

Finn looked up from closing the tractor box. "Stalking?"

"No, *stocking*. As in Christmas stockings."

Gramps rolled his eyes as if he found the whole idea of her little deliveries silly, which Amelia supposed was his way of dealing with the fact that he could no longer help with what she knew had been one of his favorite holiday traditions. "Normal people would call it delivering goodies to the neighbors. Amelia calls it stocking. It's the one thing she thinks she does anonymously." He snorted. "But everybody knows it's her."

Two could play that game. Amelia rose up to her full height. "All right, Gramps." She cleared her throat. "I require Finn's assistance so that I can deliver baked goods to our neighbors under the false pretense of anonymity. Factual enough for you?"

"Well—" Gramps frowned "—when you put it that way, *stocking* does sound better."

She kissed the top of his head. "My point exactly." She shifted her gaze to Finn, who looked reluctant to be involved in this little stunt no matter how it was described. "You said you got a temporary license document from Dr. Searle's office. I figured a short, slow tour of the neighborhood might be the perfect way for you to get behind the wheel again. Doc said you only had to wait ten days, right?"

She knew that would seal Finn's participation. "Who could say no to that?" His smile reminded her how much she had come to enjoy his company. And that was a double blessing, because the thought of stocking alone because Gramps no longer could go with her was too sad.

"We'll be back in an hour, tops, Gramps."

"Oh, don't you worry about me," Gramps said with a touch of forced cheer that pinched Amelia's heart. Yet another adjustment, yet another activity stolen by age's frailties. "You two kids have fun and stay out of trouble."

It was what Gramps had always said when Rafe picked her up for a night out. It was what Gramps had said anytime a boy took her out in high school. Amelia hoped Finn couldn't see the heat rise to her cheeks. Thank goodness it was the middle of the afternoon rather than at night when she and Gramps had done this in years past.

Finn followed her out of the den. "I don't have to dress up or anything, do I?"

Amelia laughed that Finn would think her

capable of that level of holiday antics. "No, Finn, you're just driving the getaway car." She stopped herself just short of making a joke about law enforcement driving the getaway car. *I hate all this secrecy, Lord. Let things come out in the open between Finn and me today, please.*

Amelia dashed back into the car, breathless and laughing. "That's number twelve! Go, go, before they open the door!"

Finn applied the gas to go the fifty feet to the next drive on Amelia's block. He reached behind him to the box of twenty or so decorated bags of cookies and candy with the tag "You've been blessed! Now spread the Christmas Cheer to someone else this season!" and handed the next bag to her. "You're just a little bit nuts—you know that, don't you?" He chuckled as she plucked it from his hand. He'd tried to stay skeptical and slightly annoyed at the silly tradition, but it was impossible in the face of Amelia's obvious glee. Truth was, he spent the time watching her dash back and forth admitting to a craving for her joy.

"Best kind of nuts there is." She pointed to him. "And don't try to tell me you're not having fun, because you are."

Finn held his hands up. "Maybe just a little bit, but I'm staying in the car."

"For *now*," she teased as she opened the car door and prepared for her sprint to the door and back.

Finn made a show of scrunching down in his seat as if hiding. "For good."

He watched her bound up the sidewalk, hang the bag from the doorknob and ring the doorbell. The door opened immediately, the older woman inside laughing and pulling Amelia into a joyous hug. They talked excitedly for a few minutes before Amelia pointed to the car and gave a wave. The older woman waved at Finn, and Finn found himself smiling and waving back even as he cringed.

Amelia's world was so bright, so full of love that his own life loomed all the darker by comparison. He envied her ability to roust up so much happiness. How did she keep that sparkle, that infectious bounce of hers, when she'd seen such hard times? Luther said it was her faith. Luther also said such faith could be his for the asking. He didn't think he believed that, but it was a nice idea to ponder.

Amelia was still laughing as she walked back to the car—no need to dash this time—her smile still a mile wide. "Miss Betty catches me every year. I think she watches from the window. She's eighty-four—I should be faster than her." She leaned back in her seat, eyes glowing as she looked a him, her face more amused than foiled at being caught. "What?"

He didn't know how else to put it. "You're so... happy. All the time. No matter what."

"Oh, I wouldn't say that."

"I would. There's more than enough to pull your spirits down this year and yet you're still out there making other people happy. Her—" he nodded to the door Amelia had just left "—Gramps, all those kids." He should have said *me*, but he couldn't bring himself to do it.

"Like I said, it's the best way to get over your own hurts." She spoke it with the quiet certainty of truth, yet he still couldn't quite see how the exchange took place. He'd spent all this time helping Amelia help people, and his own problems still threatened to swallow him whole.

No, that wasn't quite true. When he was with Amelia helping people, he did feel a tiny bit of the hollow sting go away. Only it wasn't about Amelia's benevolence; it was about Amelia. The ache to be near her was the one sure thing in his life right now, and there were reasons why that wasn't a good thing.

"That Rafe broke your heart but good, didn't he?"

Finn watched the pain of the subject wash over her features. "Yes, he did."

He had to tell her. It was the only obstacle he

could place between them to block the constant pull he felt toward her. "Amelia, I have to tell you something. I'm a Ranger. Was, at least. I think I still am. I'm with the force just like Rafe was."

She leaned her head back against the seat, eyes closed, absorbing what he'd just told her. There, he'd done it. Put the necessary wedge between them so that whatever he felt—whatever he suspected she felt as well—couldn't go any further.

"Thank you." Her voice was small and quiet. *Thank you?* "For what?"

"For telling me."

Only Amelia Klondike could find a way to offer thanks for an additional wound to her heart. He could tell himself he hadn't just hurt her, but with so much truth missing, now wasn't the time to start lying to himself. Best to simply get on with things. He went to put the car back into gear, but she reached out a hand to stop him. His body reacted to her touch the way it always did. Would her touch ever stop thundering through him like that? Amelia pulled her hand back, aware of what she'd done.

"I have something to tell you," she said. She caught his eyes for a brief moment before lowering her gaze in what looked like embarrassment.

He couldn't think of anything Amelia needed to be embarrassed about. "What?"

"I knew."

Finn turned to her. "You knew?"

Her cheeks turned pink. Finn thought it might be ten years before that particular shade of pink left his memory, if ever. "I overheard you talking to Gramps. I'm not proud of that, and I owe you an apology."

She'd overheard him confessing to Luther how he'd been unable to tell her about being a Ranger and *she* was apologizing to *him*? It struck Finn that even if there wasn't a single obstacle between them, he'd never deserve someone as good-hearted as Amelia. Not in a million years. "I couldn't work up the nerve to tell you. Not after what you told me about Rafe."

"I know. I heard the whole conversation, Finn. I should have walked away, but I didn't."

That meant she'd heard everything. The way he'd praised her to her grandfather, the way Luther had talked about her faith, she'd heard all of it. It hung unspoken in the air between them just now, and his chest stung from the exposure. The car felt too small, and the half-dozen bags yet to be delivered loomed like a Herculean burden instead of a silly, happy task. How did she always get so much closer to him than he wanted?

"Gramps is right, you know. God is always watching over us. And you're wrong—I'm not always happy. But I always have joy, and that's how I keep going. Happy comes and goes—" she rolled her eyes a bit "—mostly goes, at least this past year, but joy is a gift of the Spirit. Something you can ask for, like Gramps said."

"Like faith. Like healing." Finn couldn't quite believe such words were coming out of his mouth. She smiled at his response, that bone-deep, glowing smile of hers that took the sting out of anything. *Tell her.* He felt a nearly irresistible urge to tell her what he'd been doing this whole time they'd been "stocking"—something he'd never expected to admit to anyone, especially not her. "I have been." The words ought to be simple but they tangled up on his tongue. He twisted to face her fully. "While you were up at those doors, I've been sitting here asking." It wasn't anything as clear as praying, nothing close to the eloquent, heartfelt prayers Amelia and Luther said before meals. It was more of sending his hurt and hunger up to heaven in wordless pleas. "I watched you and asked God for what you had. What you and Luther have. I can't pray like you and he do, but…" He ran out of words to try to explain the unexplainable.

"Oh, Finn." Her hand covered his hand, and Finn didn't have enough distance to fight the connection it made. She understood. He was so weary of keeping her at a distance. Belinda was gone, lost to him for now if not forever, and Amelia was so very real to him right now. He'd become dangerously dependent on her as a lifeline, a beacon in the storm of everything exploding around him. Soon enough, his memory would fully return and thrust him back into his sorry, solitary life. He'd miss this glimpse of joy, the warmth that came with being near Amelia. It made the urge to grab it and keep it now that much harder to resist. If she'd only stop looking at him with all that "if only" in her eyes. It was unwinding the last shred of his resistance. *I'll only hurt you*, he wanted to shout, but watched his left hand close over hers instead.

His hand with the watch on his wrist. The watch Belinda had given him, the tangible reminder of all the terrible facts and sad history piled up like a mountain between them. They both stared at their joined hands, and Finn knew they both saw not only his hand on hers, but the watch and all it represented—their whole surreal relationship played out in one tiny scene. For a long moment Finn wrestled with the twin urges to pull her close and let her head fall against his shoulder, or to get out of the car and run until he fell over.

The way he could hear Amelia's quick breaths, she stood on the same edge—and knowing that only made everything worse. She slid her hand from underneath his and placed a single finger on the watch. "Look at the time," she said softly.

"We'd better keep going or we'll be late to get ready for supper."

With a dual stab of regret and relief, Finn felt the wonder of the moment slide away to be swallowed up by the demands of real life. Their individual lives—lives becoming more separate with every memory—would eventually split apart for good. Hadn't someone told him once that while you pray for what you want, God gives you what you need?

Chapter Thirteen

Amelia hadn't even set out the main dish that night and dinner with Boone and Lizzie was already sliding into disaster. She reapplied her smile as she removed the chicken from the oven and set it in the center of the table. She'd thought one large roaster would be enough for four adults, but just the salad had shown Boone to be a ravenous eater. "I'm glad you like my cooking, Boone," she said as she watched the young man wolf down food as if he hadn't eaten for months. His shaggy auburn hair and lean build even made him look a bit like a wild animal. Still, Boone had dashing blue-green eyes—Lizzie had always fallen for striking eyes—and a wide, bright grin.

"Seems like Boone's always starving," Lizzie said, smiling at her fiancé as if his ravenous appetite was a virtue. "I reckon our grocery bills will be sky-high once we're married."

Amelia had just had the same thought, and by Finn's expression as he caught her eye, she wasn't alone.

"Your cooking is awfully good," Finn complimented as he wisely passed the chicken to Gramps first—had Boone been given first dibs, there might be nothing left for the rest of them. "What do you do, Boone?"

"Do?" Boone wiped up the last of his salad dressing with another biscuit.

Amelia caught a momentary "is this guy for real?" spark in Finn's eye before he expounded, "Where do you work? What's your field?"

"Me? I mostly just pick up work here and there wherever I can."

"Boone's a freelance ranch hand," Lizzie said.

Now, that's a very shiny way to say Boone doesn't have a steady job, Amelia thought but kept her mouth shut. Every young person had to start out somewhere, and it wasn't as if Lizzie needed Boone's salary to support herself. Amelia had always considered her financial independence to be one of the great blessings of her life, and had tried to teach her little sister the same.

"I go where the work takes me," Boone said.

"That can do a fellow fine for a time," Gramps offered as he filled his plate with chicken before passing it to Amelia. "Hard work's good for a soul. But what would you like to do in the long run?"

"I'm not much for long-term plans, Mr. Klondike. I like to think of myself as a man of opportunity." He flashed the boyish, engaging grin Lizzie always raved about.

Amelia swallowed a large gulp of iced tea, watching the look that flashed between Gramps and Finn. Gramps had not yet invited Boone to call him Luther. "Flexibility can be a fine thing in a young man," she offered, taking only one slice of chicken as she passed the plate to Lizzie. "I expect you've learned a lot about all different kinds of ranching that way. And you must be doing well to get that fine new truck out there." Boone and Lizzie had pulled up in a shiny black top-of-the-line pickup.

"Isn't it snazzy?" Lizzie beamed. She'd always been swayed by a fancy car. Amelia didn't know much about trucks, but this one looked as if it had every bell and whistle on the market, and was so large she could probably park her little SUV in the payload.

"Sure is," Gramps offered, not bothering to keep the note of suspicion out of his words. Evidently Amelia wasn't the only one to wonder how a "freelance ranch hand" could afford such an expensive vehicle. Surely Lizzie wouldn't be so foolish as to mingle her finances with a man she hadn't yet married? Gramps had given both of them a thorough education on how to be wise with the considerable assets Mama and Daddy had left them. She'd try to catch a moment alone with Lizzie after supper and make sure those lessons had sunk in.

Amelia tried to change the subject. "Speaking of fancy, I heard some top-of-the-line boots and chaps showed up at the Larson place yesterday."

"Yeah," Boone said with another wide smile. "Can you believe all that? I think it's great that Christmas is coming early for some of the folks around here who really need it. I'd sure like to know who is doing all these crazy things." He winked at Amelia. "You sure it's not you, Miss K? My Lizzie says you got the biggest heart in the county and I don't know anybody who likes Christmas more."

Amelia would have enjoyed the compliment if it hadn't felt so…forced. He couldn't be deflecting suspicion away from himself, could he? Boone had worked at many of the ranches that had been hit. It made a disturbing sort of sense that he could be the Robin Hood, and Amelia didn't like how easily she could see him committing the crimes. He'd not been kind in his opinions of many of Little Horn's more prosperous ranchers—and he'd have knowledge of their properties and possessions.

What, then, of the other side of Little Horn's Robin Hood? Boone certainly hadn't shown a generous side with Lizzie, but could it be because Lizzie was well-off and he was helping out others who weren't? Amelia stared at him, calling on her famous intuition to tell her more about Boone. *I just don't see it in him. Am I missing something, Lord?* Amelia was rarely wrong about people, but this would be a happy beginning if she were. If he had money for such a truck, he surely must have some source of funds to be secretly generous. Perhaps it was further proof that the whole family needed to put in an effort to get to know Boone better.

Lizzie broke her chain of thought. "Speaking of new shoes, look at Boone's new boots—aren't they smart?"

At Lizzie's insistence, Boone hoisted his long leg to show of a very elaborate hand-tooled cowboy boot. If Boone was buying gifts, he was certainly including himself on the list. Fond of shoes as Amelia was, it didn't take long to calculate that the set of boots on Boone's feet probably rivaled the tiny diamond on Lizzie's left hand. Where was the lavish generosity to the woman he loved? "Very fancy indeed," Amelia said. She swallowed her irritation that Boone seemed to be quick to spend funds on himself but enjoyed his fiancée's "financial independence." Lizzie clearly was over the moon for her man and had bought him many gifts, but Boone didn't seem to dote on his soon-to-be bride in the way Amelia would have wanted for her sister.

"Boone, how do you like the wedding plans so far?" She watched for Boone's face to light up at the prospect of his upcoming wedding.

"Lizzie's got us signed up for that class at your church." His tone was decidedly neutral; neither thrilled nor annoyed. And he'd said *your church*—not *our church*.

Amelia diverted her attention to Gramps and Finn. Gramps's face was pleasant enough, but Amelia hoped Lizzie and Boone couldn't see the skeptical edges in Gramps's eyes. The evening was definitely not taking the "warm up to Boone" atmosphere she'd hoped. And Finn? He just kept staring out the window at the truck in the driveway. Was he having the same thoughts about Boone's new purchases? Or was he just uncomfortable as the only nonfamily member in this family gathering? It struck her—and not in a good way—that Finn seemed to fit in around the table far better than Boone did. *That's not fair*, Amelia reminded herself. *It's Lizzie's heart that chose Boone, not yours.*

And just what was her heart doing in regard to Finn Brannigan? Could she chide Lizzie for her a lack of wisdom when she was showing a growing lack herself? There had been a moment back in the car, a long moment when their hands had touched, when her heart had turned over in her chest and woken up in a way she hadn't thought possible. At least not possible for a long time since the wounds of Rafe's departure. The practicalities of life didn't let her trust that current longing. Finn was handsome, kind and well-mannered—all the things she currently found lacking in Boone—but he was also deeply troubled, full of uncertainties and most of all quite likely bound to another woman who missed him very much. And now she knew he was also in the same profession that had pulled Rafe from her.

Were I to make a list of pros and cons, Amelia thought to herself, for it was something Mama had taught her to do when making a hard decision, *the "con" column would be filled.*

Ah, but Mama also taught her to trust her instincts and the Spirit's nudging. Sometimes, Mama had said, you only needed one "pro." In fact, some of her best successes at Here to Help had been the illogical long shots.

And that's my problem, Amelia thought as she allowed herself a long look at Finn while he politely asked Boone about the features of his truck. *I've been taught to believe in long shots.*

* * *

The truck had been driving him crazy all night. Finn couldn't stop staring at it, couldn't shake the bad feeling it gave him. Had he owned one just like it? Was that the connection? A low hum of panic had started in his stomach at dinner and hadn't let up yet. Not to mention his reaction to this Boone fellow. He didn't want to be rude and had no business passing judgment, but the guy gave him a distinctly bad feeling. The kind of gut instinct Finn imagined a Ranger both fine-tuned and relied upon—the "bad guy" opposite of Amelia's spiritual nudge to see the best in people.

He caught Boone's elbow as everyone but Boone rose from the table when Lizzie and Amelia went seeing to dessert—pie, of course. Didn't this man's mama teach him to stand up when a woman left the table? He didn't remember his past, but at least he could remember his manners, for crying out loud. "Hey, Boone, you mind if I take a closer look at that impressive truck of yours?"

"Uh…I suppose," Boone said, starting to rise.

"No, don't get up—stay with your lady." Finn wanted a chance to look at the truck without Boone watching. He needed to find out what about this truck set his skin to prickling.

Had he once had a bad experience with a black pickup? He knew from the files Dr. Searle gave him that his wife had been driving a light blue hatchback when she'd been killed. He stood still in the hallway for a moment, waiting for a wall of pain to hit him as he tried to remember the death of his wife and child. Again, a wave of hollow, factual regret washed over him, but it was an empty grief for facts he couldn't yet feel. He shut his eyes and leaned against the front door. *I'm sorry, Belinda. I'm so sorry, Annie. I will remember you—somehow—I promise.*

To his surprise, the vow was followed easily by a prayer. *I can't go on like this, Lord. You've got to give me my memory back. I can't stand it. I'll gladly swallow all the pain if You'll just heal me.*

The fancy truck fairly gleamed in the sunset, large and imposing. A real "look at me" vehicle, full of chrome and dark windows. It looked like the kind of car a guy would keep spotless, but the truck was splotched with mud and even some bits of shrub from a recent off-road adventure. He peeked in the driver's side window— tinted, of course—to see fast-food bags and a handful of shirts strewn all over the passenger seat. He hadn't even moved the shirts for Lizzie to sit when they'd driven here together, for crying out loud. Manners or not, Finn felt as if he'd have a hard time keeping his mouth shut if Amelia asked him what he really thought of Boone.

The truck bed showed the same sloppy care, with shovels, a box or two and several tools just tossed in. It was the cable cutter that caught Finn's suspicious eye—just the kind of tool to clip cattle fencing. Had Boone made it onto Lucy Benson's list of suspects for the rustler plaguing Little Horn? If not, he ought to be.

It was the far side of the car, however, that dropped a rock into Finn's stomach. A large scrape on the front passenger-side fender, ending in a dent. The side of a black pickup truck wasn't a unique sight—Little Horn must have two dozen trucks something like it driving around town. Still, this truck made Finn's pulse raise. It was a big truck, dark and powerful, but even that didn't explain Finn's physical reaction to the vehicle. Honestly, it felt as if the thing was coming at him, even parked as it was. He stood off to the right side of the truck, staring at it and the dent, telling himself there was no rational explanation for what he was feeling.

The flash of image came at him like a lightning strike, nearly knocking the wind out of him. A black pickup—large and tricked-out like this one—barreling down a dirt road right at him. He could feel his eyes squinting in the blinding headlights, remember the gravel slipping under his feet as he ran. He could hear the rumble of the souped-up exhaust as the truck sped up, see the reflection of his frightened face in the tinted windows as the metal slammed him in the ribs.

Finn fell against the car, gasping for breath at the onslaught of memory, and then pulled away to stare in shock at the dent in the car. It matched the height of his shoulder. He grabbed on to the large rearview mirror the same way he had done in his memory, frightened to find the smear of a handprint in the exact position where his fingers now lay.

It wasn't possible, was it? This could not be the car in his memory. His whole body shook as he remembered the impact, remembered the feeling of his arms and legs tumbling around him as he rolled down the hillside toward pine trees. Hadn't Amelia said he was found under some pine trees?

His body had to be drawing connections that weren't there; the trauma was running away with his imagination. Still, the bruises that were just fading on his shoulder, the pain that still lingered on the left side of his ribs—those things weren't in his imagination.

Ducking toward the back of the truck, Finn began rummaging through the items in the payload searching for anything that looked familiar. It was impulsive, assumptive even, but he couldn't stop himself. He pulled to toolbox toward him and flipped the lid, sucking in a breath at a black ski mask with orange trim—the kind hunters used—wadded up in the top tray. *I know that mask. I've seen it.*

A dozen men could own that mask, he argued with himself, but the alarms in his brain continued to go off. He could see the figure—flannel shirt, ripped blue jeans, dark brown gloves... and black ski mask. A tall, lanky guy just about Boone's height.

Get a hold of yourself, man. You can't be sure of anything. You don't even know if what you remember is real. Finn's hands went up over his eyes again, the desperate feeling of his composure sliding away rising back up over him the way it had in the hospital. *Calm down. You can't walk back in there like this.*

He heard the front door open and Bug's scrambling paws come down the driveway. Finn pulled himself together just in time to quietly latch the toolbox shut and walk forward to meet Boone's grin over the hood of the car.

"Pretty, ain't she?"

Boone's voice sounded smooth and sinister even as Finn told himself he had no proof of the suspicion clanging through his brain right now. "Fine thing," he choked out, feeling as if he'd swallowed a handful of dust. "Let me hear how she fires up, will you?" he asked as calmly as he could.

"No different than any other," Boone said. Was that resistance Finn heard in his voice?

"Looks like you had the exhaust refitted special," Finn persisted, pulling open the driver's side door for Boone. "I reckon she roars like a lion." *I'm sure I know* exactly *how she does.* He stood back, Bug circling beside him, and waited for the sound to hit him in the way he knew it would. *I'll go to my grave with that sound in my ears*, he thought. It had come back to him with such grisly clarity that he felt as if he could pick it out of a hundred vehicles on a racetrack.

The truck roared to life, sending Bug running for the side yard and sending Finn's gut down through the soles of his shoes. There was no mistaking the deep, throaty roar of this truck's exhaust.

You hit me, Finn wanted to roar above the rumble. *You did this to me.* He wanted to climb in the cab and punch Boone's jaw. Finn felt his fingers flex with the overwhelming urge to make Boone pay for all the pain, all the frustration, all the unknowing of the past two weeks with some pain of his own. Only the knowledge that Amelia and Lizzie could see the truck through the kitchen windows kept his raging temper in check. He couldn't be sure yet—there wasn't enough proof to lash out and there certainly wasn't enough proof to call Lucy Benson. He needed something more substantial than his unreliable memory. *Not here*, he repeated to himself until his throat unclenched. *Not now. But soon.*

"When you boys are done playing with your big, shiny toys, there's pie and coffee" came Amelia's voice from the front door.

"It's okay, Miss K," Boone called as he quickly killed the ignition. "We're done here."

Oh, no, we're not, Finn thought as he called Bug to his side. He picked up the chubby little dog so he would have an excuse not to look Boone in the eyes right now. *I haven't even gotten started with you.*

Chapter Fourteen

Amelia grabbed Lucy's arm on the way out of Bible study at the Little Horn Community Church Wednesday morning. "Have you got time for coffee?"

Lucy smiled. "Didn't we just drink coffee and eat coffee cake?"

In Lucy's defense, delicious snacks were one of the best parts of the women's Bible study Amelia attended twice a month, but this wasn't about refreshments. "I could use a friendly ear."

"Oh," Lucy said. "*That* kind of coffee." She pulled out her smartphone, squinting at it for a second before announcing, "I've got forty minutes. Fifty if you want to ride out with me to pick up some files at the county office. I've been meaning to ask you how things have been going anyway."

"Let's drive. I don't really need more coffee

anyway." She climbed into the passenger seat of Lucy's SUV. "Let me call Gramps and let him know I'll be another hour."

Gramps picked up the phone right away. "Hi there, honey."

"I'm going to run down to the county office with Lucy for an hour or so. You'll be okay until I get back?"

Gramps chuckled. "I'm fine. Finn's here, re-member. And boy, will you be surprised when you see what he's been up to."

Amelia gulped. "Surprised how?"

"Now, if I told you, it wouldn't be much of a surprise, would it?" Gramps's voice was light enough, but Amelia wasn't in much of a mood to add more chaos to her already chaotic life.

"Will I like this surprise?"

"I think so. You let me know when you see it. We'll expect you in about an hour, then, but no need to hurry."

Amelia slipped the phone back into her purse and pushed out a breath.

"What was that all about?" Lucy's green eyes widened under the fringe of her blond bangs.

"Gramps said Finn has a surprise for me when I get back home."

"Well, now, maybe it is a good thing that we've got those ten extra minutes. Tell me about Finn.

I've been a little concerned since that scene in the park."

Amelia ran her fingers through a curl, deciding how to describe all that had happened since she spoke with Lucy last. "He remembers more than he's telling me, I know that. Dr. Searle gave him some papers that set him off that day. He won't say what was in them, but it was some terrible shock to him." She looked at her friend. "There's something devastating in Finn's past, Lucy. I don't know if it was something he did or something done to him, but it pulled the rug right out from underneath him, that's for sure."

Lucy pursed her lips. "Do you want me to look into it?"

Lucy wasn't quick to use her professional contacts for personal reasons, so the offer only confirmed Amelia's suspicion that Lucy still had her doubts about Finn. "No, I don't want to invade his privacy like that. The way he explained it, he knew what had happened, but he wouldn't share it until he remembered it. If you ask me, that means it's about 'B,' whoever she is. Just the way he talks, I know it's about someone very close to him."

"Have you thought about how close *you're* getting to him?" Lucy's words were gentle, but her eyes showed concern for her friend. "You're falling for him—even I can see that. Are you sure you're in a good place to be smart about that right now?"

Amelia leaned her head against the window. The morning was crisp and clear—her favorite kind of Texan winter day. "Is it that obvious?"

Shrugging, Lucy pulled out onto the highway. "Maybe only to me. There's a heap of unknowns here, Amelia. I don't want you to get hurt again. Have you considered that he may still be married to this 'B'?"

Amelia shut her eyes. "Every second of every day. Believe me, Lucy, my head knows this is a bad idea. My heart doesn't seem to want to listen. Even with all the questions, I'm comfortable with him. Finn fits better into our family than Boone does right now—how irritating is that?"

"Ah, Boone. How did the 'get to know your future brother-in-law' dinner go?"

"If you base it on the sheer volume of chicken that boy put away, it went fabulously."

Lucy laughed. "That doesn't sound like an unqualified success to me."

Turning toward Lucy, Amelia offered, "He arrived in a brand-new, very expensive truck. He's flush with money all of a sudden, Lucy, and I wonder where it came from." She hated to implicate Boone even a little, but facts were piling up against the man.

"He's worked at most of the ranches that got

hit. That would give him knowledge on how to beat their security systems."

Amelia had to ask, "He's still on your list of suspects, isn't he?" How was she ever going to break this to Lizzie? Should she even try?

"He's not my prime suspect, if that helps. I still think this other guy could be our rustler, but I haven't got enough to bring him in for questioning yet. The truck is flashy, you say?"

"As much as I know about trucks." Amelia remembered how the big black truck with all that chrome practically filled her driveway. "You sure notice it when he drives up."

"Well, even though no one has mentioned a fancy truck involved, a thief smart enough to outwit so many security cameras wouldn't flash such a noticeable vehicle around town to draw suspicion."

Amelia laughed. "Are you saying you don't think Boone is smart enough to be our Robin Hood?" She had to admit, Boone didn't strike her as the sharpest tool in the shed—certainly no match for how clever Lizzie could be when she set her mind to something. "And there's another thing—something odd went on between Boone and Finn while they were out looking at Boone's truck."

"How so?"

"I don't know how to explain it. Neither of

them said anything, but there was this prickling between them—mostly on Finn's part, I think. Boone never seems to get worked up about anything—when they came inside, Finn's face was all tight even when he tried to be pleasant, and he went up to his room right after we finished desert and didn't come down for the rest of the night."

Lucy's eyebrows furrowed. "Maybe he was just giving you, Boone, Lizzie and Gramps some time to be a family?"

"No, it's something else. Finn was trying to be nice to Boone during dinner, but after they went out to see the truck, Finn just sort of shut down. Nothing mean, just a sort of—" Amelia searched for the right description "—unsettling distance. I could see his brain going a mile a minute, but it had nothing to do with anything in the room."

"Do you think he remembered something while he was out there?"

Amelia sighed. "I can't think of any other explanation. They seemed to be talking friendly enough when I looked out there. And Finn did seem especially interested in the truck even before he asked Boone to go look at it."

"Did you ask him about it?"

"I didn't get the chance," Amelia replied. "He didn't come down for the rest of the night and he still hadn't come down when I left for Bible study this morning. I tell you, something happened out there in my driveway. I just don't know what it was."

Finn had wrestled most of the evening and the early part of this morning about what to do with Boone. The man in him knew it was Boone who had knocked him down out there on the hillside. The Ranger in him knew he couldn't prove it. If he was going to upend Amelia's family by taking his suspicions to Lucy, he needed rock-solid evidence.

By the time Amelia headed off to church, he'd made up his mind and had a plan. The trouble with that plan was that he couldn't do a single thing about it until tonight, so the waiting was driving him crazy. A conversation with Luther would probably lead to a discussion of Boone, and that was dangerous. Finn was pretty sure Luther shared his suspicions of Boone, but this was no time to tip his hand to the old man. He was better off steering clear of any Klondike for as much of the day as possible.

Any Klondike, that was, except one.

He had gotten Bug to manage half the flight of stairs this morning, egged on by a carefully placed trail of oatmeal cookies and a whole lot of encouragement. At the moment Finn was lying beside a puffing Bug in the middle of the stairs, trying to get the fat little beast up to the top.

"Come on, boy, I know you have it in you. Dig deep, you little piglet."

Finn nudged the oatmeal cookie bit a little closer off the end of the next step, watching Bug strain his thick furry neck and give a little lick. "That delicious cookie is just sitting there waiting for you. Come on." In desperation he gave the dog's rump a declarative nudge while snapping his fingers above the cookie. The combination startled Bug into action, who made two steps into a scrambling leap, then shuffled himself around to survey his new altitude with a canine mixture of fear and pride.

"Don't look down, Bug!" Finn cried, scooting up two steps to put his head even with the dog's. He'd become ridiculously invested in the chubby little guy's ascent, he knew that. It made no sense except that somewhere inside he needed a victory—any victory—and this one was the closest at hand.

"Come on, Bug, ol' boy!" came Luther's cheer from the bottom of the steps, cane brandished like a cavalry flag. "The top is yours. Get on up there for both of us!"

The last four steps loomed above him, and Finn knew he was not getting off this staircase until both he and Bug stood victoriously at its top. He snapped his fingers and gave Bug another nudge. Bug was no slouch—he'd figured out the system, and with a mighty snort, he hoisted his body up over the step to munch another bit of cookie.

"That's it. You got it now, you old hound!" Luther cried from below them. "Show us what you can do!"

Finn crawled up to the top of the stairs, not caring how absurd this whole thing must look, and fixed his gaze on Bug's bulging black eyes. The dog was panting, licking his chops for the feast of cookies before him, but he had fire in his eyes. He wanted it. Victory was within reach. "Come on, Bug. The top is waiting for you."

With a final surge of canine courage, Bug waddled, scrambled and lunged himself up to the landing, where he was lauded by two grown men cheering like idiots. Finn picked the dog up and ruffled his squat head. He handed Bug an entire cookie, not minding the drooly licks that scooped the treat from his palm.

"I'm gonna go see if we have any steak in the freezer," Luther said. "I'll grill that dog his very own for doing it. Who knows? If Bug can get upstairs, I just might be next."

Finn laughed, Luther laughed, and Finn dared anyone to argue that Bug wasn't laughing, as well. Ten minutes later, while the steak was thawing, the trio did the whole thing again—this time with oatmeal cookie bits on every other step.

While Luther fired up the grill, Finn's chest glowed with absurd pride while Bug made it all the way up the stairs for a single cookie. Bug earned every bit of the steak Luther was going to make him, and Finn felt the buoyancy of at least one solid accomplishment fill his lungs. "All hail Bug the Conqueror!" He laughed, scooping up the dog to bring him out to the patio, where his victory dinner awaited him.

Amelia came in the kitchen door just as he passed. She had every right to look as astonished as she did—he had no doubt this doggy celebration must look as if the Klondike household had lost its collective marbles.

"What on earth is going on?" She looked from Finn to Bug to Luther out on the porch brandishing a barbecue fork. "Gramps, whatever are you doing out there?"

"What does it look like I'm doing?" Luther grinned. "I'm fixin' a steak for the dog."

Amelia balked at the obviousness of that declaration, raising one blond eyebrow at Finn. "Mind explaining *why* Bug's getting steak?"

Finn put the dog down, who rushed over to his owner and began snuffling excitedly as if to announce his own accomplishment. "It'll all make sense in a minute." After she shot him an "I doubt that" look, he amended his remark to "Well, it might make *more* sense in a minute."

"That's good," she said, eyeing Luther's position at the grill with a fair amount of concern, "because it doesn't make a lick of sense at the moment."

"Go on and show her, son," Luther called from the porch. "I'll be finished up here in a minute."

Amelia's eyebrows rose and her lips pursed. "Show me what?"

Finn pulled another cookie from the Christmas-tree-shaped cookie jar, showing it to Bug, who immediately scooted to his place at the foot of the stairs. "Show you this."

He gestured to the stairs as he and Amelia followed Bug to the hallway. Finn would probably never be able to explain how he was so proud of the tubby little dog for this feat. Then again, he couldn't explain a lot about his life. It just felt so good to accomplish something, to jump just one hurdle in life, even if it wasn't his own. He pointed at Bug. "Stay, boy," he said, and then proceeded to climb to the top of the stairs and place the cookie in sight at the edge of the landing.

"You've got to be kidding me," Amelia said. Her tone was a delightful mix of disbelief and astonishment. Bug's little curly tail began to twitch, evidently as eager to show off the new skill as Finn was.

Coming back down the flight to stand beside Amelia, Finn patted Bug on the rump. "Go on, Bug. Show your mama what you can do."

Bug put his paws on the first step and began his ascent. "I don't believe it," Amelia whispered. Finn felt the astonishment in her voice tickle down the back of his neck. "Can he?"

"Twice today," Finn whispered, crazy pride puffing up his chest.

With a series of snuffles and scrambles, Bug worked his way up five of the twelve steps. Finn felt every single step, astonished to realize he'd been holding his breath. It was a dog, for crying out loud. A fat, adorable, brave little dog. Maybe Amelia had every right to think the Klondike household had lost its senses.

Bug turned with one paw on the sixth step, as if to make sure everyone was watching. The dog actually looked nervous—which couldn't possibly be true, but those big eyes were so comically expressive Finn couldn't help but be nervous for the beast. "Go on, Bug, smell that steak grilling and be a champ."

As he turned back to his ascent, Bug lost his footing and slipped back down one step. Amelia gasped and lunged for the dog, but Finn caught her and held her back by both shoulders. "No, he's okay. He can do this." The move brought them close, and when Amelia turned to look at him with that "I've got to help" plea in her eyes, something unwound in Finn's chest. Some tightly coiled knot that had begun to loose back in the car slipped out of his control. "You don't have to help him," he said, the tender tone of his voice sounding as if it belonged on some other man. "He's going to be fine."

Bug kicked and scrambled his hind legs back up onto the fifth step, and Finn felt Amelia leaning toward the dog. He held on to her shoulders, noting how the top of her hair brushed his chin and the rosy smell of whatever scent she wore. He was looking at the dog but noticing every detail of how close they were. She was looking at Bug as well, but by the catch in her breath and the tension in her shoulders, he knew it was the same for her.

Bug settled himself on the sixth step, and then the seventh, and Finn knew he ought to let go of Amelia but didn't. "Seven," she called in the gently encouraging tone that for now was his first memory. "Come on, boy, eight."

As Bug moved from the ninth stair to the tenth, Amelia's hand came up to cover Finn's on her shoulder. The feel of her small hand atop his opened up some wide space under Finn's ribs, the knotted spot all but gone. For the first time in all he could remember, he felt like a normal man again, not some kind of walking disaster.

She turned to look at Finn, and he felt everything a normal man would feel in the astonished gaze of a beautiful woman.

At the moment, for a split second he wanted to freeze and keep forever, Finn's heart didn't feel dead, nor did it feel locked down and lost. He hadn't forgotten how to care for a woman. He knew, right then with her eyes sparkling in excitement for the same absurd victory that glowed in his own chest, that "forgotten" was not the same thing as "gone." Not at all.

Bug's "woof" pulled their eyes back to the stairway, where he sat alternately gobbling up the cookie and running in excited circles around the top landing. "You've done it!" she cried, rising up on tiptoes to throw her arms around Finn's neck in delight.

There was no hesitation in how his arms slipped around her waist to hold her close. It was like walking out of a dark room into a burst of sunlight, and the feel of her tight against him cracked some internal shell that had bound him to darkness. *This*, his brain told him in the sloweddown potency of the moment, *is what they mean when they say holding on to hope*. He hadn't even recognized how hopeless he'd become until this woman and her silly little dog gave it back to him.

Chapter Fifteen

❧

"This was the big surprise? I didn't know what to expect, but it sure wasn't this. It's like the little guy is in training for Mount Everest," Lucy admired as she and Amelia stood at the bottom of the stairs Thursday afternoon. Silly as it was, Amelia couldn't resist showing off Bug's new accomplishments. "He'll be fighting trim by Valentine's Day if he keeps this up."

"That's if we can get him to do it without the oatmeal-cookie finish line," Amelia admitted. "And no more steak."

"Did you really cook this dog a victory steak?" Lucy called into the den, where Gramps sat reading in his recliner.

"What? Are you going to arrest me for it, Sheriff?" Gramps called back. Lucy and Gramps always found opportunities to tease each other.

"No, sir. I was just wondering what I'd get if *I* climbed the stairs."

Gramps rumpled his newspaper. "My best smile."

Amelia laughed, and Lucy pointed a finger at Bug as he made his way down the staircase. "It's clear who got the better of this deal. You always were a charmer, Bug." Then in a soft voice, Lucy added, "Speaking of charmers, where's Finn?"

Amelia headed for the kitchen, keeping this conversation away from Gramps. "I let him borrow my car for the afternoon to go to his final appointment with Dr. Searle."

"He can drive now?"

"He faxed his police report down to the Department of Motor Vehicles and they mailed him a temporary document care of Dr. Searle. He picked it up a few days ago."

Lucy stared at her with an odd expression.

"What?" Amelia asked, worried by Lucy's response.

"The DMV requires a verifiable mailing address. Any document they sent him would show that address. So if he has it, Finn knows where he lives. He can go home."

Amelia sank into one of her kitchen chairs. "I hadn't thought of that." He'd told her about the paperwork, but hadn't shown it to her.

Lucy put her hand on Amelia's arm. "So you

have to ask yourself why? Why hasn't he gone home?"

Lucy was right; Finn knew his address now. He had what he needed to go back to his own life—and had known for a few days. The facts told her what her own heart already knew: Finn hadn't left because he wasn't ready to leave— and not in the medical sense. The same way she knew yesterday, when he held her for that long moment during Bug's stair climb, that she didn't want him to leave. She didn't want Finn to pull himself out of her life and go back to his.

There wasn't any point in pretending—especially not with Lucy. "I don't think he wants to go." She paused for a moment before daring to add, "And I don't want him to go." Amelia put her hand on her chest, an unsettling combination of panic and awareness throwing her off balance. "I don't want him to go, Lucy. I'm falling for him. There's a dozen reasons why it won't work, but... but I'm falling for him. Hard."

She waited for the lecture Lucy was sure to deliver. She'd deserve every word of it, too. Lucy closed her eyes and pushed out a breath. "Amelia, heaven knows I want you to be happy. I don't want to see you hurt again. And I'm not saying Finn couldn't be the guy to make you happy, but there are so many questions. Why he hasn't told you where he lives if he knows? I hate to be the one to ask this but, Amelia, don't you wonder what else has hasn't told you?"

"Of course I do." The words felt weak on her tongue. She'd been pretending he wasn't keeping things from her. Which was silly—he'd already told her he knew more than he was saying. Could she believe his story about wanting to sort it out for himself before sharing? Or was her heart running off with her better judgment?

"You need Finn to be straight with you before this goes any further. There might be a logical explanation, but you had better know what it is right now."

Lucy was right, of course. Everything she'd felt there at the bottom of the staircase—and all the other places she'd fought off the strong connection growing between them—couldn't override all the questions.

"If he really cares for you, he'll be honest with you. You know that. Rafe may have had his priorities all wrong, but he never deceived you. Don't let Finn string you along just because it feels good to help him. I know you're the one who found him in the woods, but remember, we still don't even know how he got there."

Amelia let her head sink into her hands. "This is all such a mess. I don't know what to do."

Lucy's hand came to rest on her shoulder. "Yes, you do. I'll stay here if you want. I'll be with you when you ask him if that's what you need. I'll go run his name through the system if that'll help."

A background check on Finn Brannigan as if he were some kind of criminal? Amelia's stomach turned at the thought. "No. I don't want that. If I can't hear it from Finn himself, it won't matter what I learn through that system of yours. I'd rather hear terrible news straight from him than good news from detective work."

Amelia straightened in her chair. She was a Klondike. If she couldn't trust Finn on her own, there was no point in trusting him at all. She was starting to glimpse Finn's heart, seeing the true man underneath all the trauma. If she couldn't count on her intuition to tell her if Finn was deceiving her now, when could she? "You don't need to stay. I'll ask him to tell me everything. I'll just have to trust that God will help me handle what I hear."

Lucy pulled her into a tight hug. "You can handle anything. You're the strongest person I know. But even the strongest people can let their heart get in the way of good sense. If you don't need me there when you talk to him, will you promise to tell me what Finn tells you?"

That felt like a violation of privacy, but then again, Amelia knew her objectivity regarding Finn was fast slipping out of her fingers. "So you're going to go all 'sheriff' on me?" Amelia held on to the hug, grateful for a friend like Lucy, one willing to say the hard things when they needed saying.

Lucy pushed back to hold Amelia at arm's length. "Just this once."

As she said goodbye to Lucy, Amelia settled into her favorite chair with a cup of coffee and her Bible. The worn book lay unopened on her lap as she closed her eyes and let her head fall back against the soft cushions, feeling Bug settle down at her feet the way he always did when she spent time with God. Gramps, who'd been a high school chemistry teacher, always teased that Bug got his faith by "osmosis"—the process of one chemical seeping from one solution into another. Feeling the rhythm of Bug's panting chest against her feet, it wasn't so hard to believe.

I know You sent Finn into my life, Lord, but I can't yet see why. I can't stand to be hurt again—You know that. And Finn seems like he's dragging so much pain around. You see my heart, You see what I feel for Finn. And You see Finn's heart, too. Only You know what's best here. I know I can trust that, but I'm all mixed-up inside. I don't even know what to pray for, except that You work all this out to Your purposes. When Finn comes back, give me the strength to ask him everything I need to ask. And help me cope with the answers, whatever they are.

* * *

"Physically, you are in good shape," Dr. Searle said as he closed his file. "Mentally and emotionally, I want to recommend—again—that you talk to someone who can help you sort this out. You Ranger types are quick to tout your strengths, but getting help in such an extreme situation as this isn't a sign of weakness."

"I hear you." Finn's acknowledgment wasn't an agreement, and Dr. Searle's eyes showed he recognized the difference. "Thank you for all your help."

Searle sat back in his chair. "So you're leaving? Going back to Austin now that you have an address?"

If only it were that simple. "I don't know yet." For starters, he didn't have a car, and there was no way Finn was leaving Little Horn with this business of Boone unsettled. And then there was Amelia. He still had no idea what to do about her and what to tell her—if he told her anything.

"Do you remember Belinda and Annie yet? Anything from your life as a Ranger?"

Finn wiped his hands down his face. "I get bits of things—more like impressions than anything I'd call a memory. But no. I look at those photos and they're strangers. I have to go back, Doc. I'm pretty sure it's the only way."

"You don't sound eager to go home."

Finn scratched his chin. "I'm pretty sure it's gonna be awful when it all comes back to me. Much as I hate the numbness, part of me is grateful for it, you know?"

"All the more reason I wish you'd talk to someone. It doesn't even have to someone from your old Company at Waco. It can be someone from the headquarters office right there in Austin."

Finn didn't see how baring his soul for dissection by some total stranger was going to do him any good. "It's not like the facts are going to change. My family is gone. I don't remember them. And when I do, they'll still be gone."

"Have you considered staying in Little Horn for a while? You have friends here, friends you may need as you work through this. Even under the best of circumstances, the holidays can be rough with a recent loss, much less one the size of yours." Searle leaned in. "I'm speaking as a friend now, not a neurologist. I wish you'd stay."

It never ceased to amaze Finn how quickly people in Little Horn called him friend. Even Carson Thorn, whom Finn had met all of twice, greeted him as if they were longtime buddies. It would be so easy to hide from his past in a place like this, but Finn knew it wouldn't solve anything.

"Thanks for that, but my life isn't here. I think the only thing I can do is go back to Austin and try to dig up whatever is left of my life and go on."

Dr. Searle frowned—Finn hadn't succeeded in hiding the hopelessness that proposition gave him. Finn couldn't remember exactly what was waiting for him back in Austin, but it didn't take a genius to know it was empty compared to his last few weeks in Little Horn.

Finn stood and picked up the set of final papers Searle had laid out for him. "If it counts for anything, my memories of Little Horn will be good ones. And hey, that's not such a bad thing right now, since they're my only memories, huh?"

The doctor stood and offered a hand. "Take care of yourself, Finn. God be with you."

Finn only nodded. If God was going to follow him back to Austin, Finn wasn't sure the Almighty would like what He found.

Chapter Sixteen

The afternoon came and went without Finn's return. "The man has barely been alone since you found him," Gramps offered to Amelia's rising concerns. "He's probably just taking some time to sort things out."

Even Gramps's consolation, however, wore thin as the afternoon turned to evening, and supper held an empty place at the table. Just as she was clearing the plates, the phone rang and Amelia jumped to answer it.

"Amelia?"

"Finn?" She was a bit shocked—but not unhappy—to hear his voice. "Are you all right?"

"I got my accounts straightened out at the bank and replaced my cell phone. It took a while longer than I thought."

He was putting the pieces of his life back together. She shouldn't be surprised, but the evidence of his leaving her dropped into her stomach like a ball of ice. "That's okay," she said, hating how the words sounded exactly like what she would say to Rafe when he called her to tell her he'd have to postpone a date.

She had to ask, "Where are you?"

He hesitated to answer, which told Amelia more than his words. "I'm in Austin."

"Austin?" The city was nearly two hours away. Why had he gone so far?

"I promise to refill your gas tank but I… I had some things I had to do."

She felt as if she could feel him leaving even now, hear his voice slipping farther away through the phone connection. "Are you all right?" she asked again, realizing he hadn't answered her the first time.

"I'm going to be a while longer. I just wanted you to know that."

So many times she'd heard that—or something just like it—from Rafe. The familiarity ran cold down her back and cut sharp edges into her words. "Thank you."

He must have heard the change in her tone, for she could hear him him push out a breath. In her imagination she could see him putting one hand over his eyes the way he did when frustrated or overwhelmed. "I am coming back, Amelia."

Of course he had to come back—he had to

return her car. But whatever had been pulled tight between them all afternoon had just snapped, and she felt the distance growing already. He might be returning, but not for long. She pulled in a steadying breath. "Take whatever time you need but, Finn, we need to talk when you get here."

"I know. I owe you that. And I'm going to try to be ready." There was a long pause before he said, "Say a few prayers for me, will you?"

If there was any request that could break her heart a little more, he'd just made it. Amelia realized, as she blinked back tears, that she'd fallen head over heels for Finn and was going to have to watch him walk out of her life. *Oh, Father, I'm not sure I have it in me.* She gave the most truthful answer she could. "How about I pray for both of us?"

Gramps, who had been rinsing dishes at the counter, stood still and stared at her.

"You do that. I shouldn't be too much longer."

Amelia had always wondered what it would feel like to wait up as Rafe's wife, dozing in a chair and saying prayers until the garage door opened and the man she cared about returned home to safety. Somehow she knew tonight would be her only time to keep such a vigil. Maybe it was a fitting goodbye after all. "Just be safe."

Finn clicked off the connection, and Amelia stared at the phone in her hands for a moment, the dial tone of the ended call sounding like a lonesome echo.

"Darlin'?" Gramps asked softly, a tender concern in his eyes.

"This is what Rangers do, isn't it?" Amelia said as she put the phone back in place. "Disappear for long stretches with no word? I should be used to it by now."

Grandpa sighed and opened the sink drain to let the water out. "So he did finally tell you. He knew you'd be hurt by it. He was trying to find a way to tell you." Gramps picked up his cane from where it was leaning against the kitchen counter and walked over to her. "He's hung up something fierce on you, you know that? And don't think I don't know you're hung up something fierce on him. I was young once, too, remember? I ain't so old that I've forgotten what that looks like."

The Christmas carol kitchen clock—one of Amelia's favorite decorations—chimed eight o'clock, which for this clock meant a music-box version of "Away in a Manger." It brought back the stormy blue torment in Finn's eyes that night at the food-truck court. Those eyes that could show so much light and shadow at the same time. "What does that change, Gramps? He's been to his home now. He's putting his old life back together, with all the people in it." Amelia felt a surprising pang of jealousy for B, whomever she was. Still, if B was important to him, why was he hesitating to return home? Where were all the people waiting to welcome the long-lost Finn Brannigan back into their lives?

"Are you sure?" Grandpa put one hand in his pocket, jingling his change the way he always did when thinking. "Didn't you tell me Finn said he felt as if he was a very lonely man in his old life?"

"I know he said that, but…"

"So would a man with a family so glad to have him return be calling to tell you he'll be back?"

Gramps had a point. "Who is 'B' and where is she?"

"I don't know. Seems to me that's something you'll have to ask Finn when he comes here."

Amelia leaned back against the counter. "There are a lot of things I have to ask Finn when he gets here."

"Oh, I agree." He pulled Amelia into a gentle hug. "But will you take an old man's advice?"

"Sure, Gramps." Even at thirty, she could become a little girl in Gramps's arms, wanting him to "make it all better."

"With all the facts you get out of that man, make sure to ask how he feels about you. Some things are just as important as facts—maybe even more important, if you ask me."

* * *

Finn sat behind the wheel at the intersection of the highway that led into Little Horn, feeling stripped out and hollow. He'd been to the Austin address listed as his apartment and found it a bare, dark maze of rooms—a lifeless box compared to the cluttered joy of Amelia's home. After an hour, he'd had to leave his own home; suffocated by the vaguely familiar yet foreign emptiness of the place.

Now he sat at the turn into Little Horn, trying to make his hand flip the turn signal on, summoning up the will to pull Amelia's car back into her driveway and put an end to his stay in Little Horn. He hadn't lied to Amelia—he was coming back—he just couldn't come back *to stay.* Not when he couldn't give her what she wanted, what she deserved. Instead, he found himself sitting on the shoulder of the intersection, watching all the ordinary cars go about their happy holiday tasks.

He touched the sparkly little Christmas stocking that swung from Amelia's rearview mirror and smiled. Even her car didn't escape decoration. A tractor trailer went by all lit up with holiday lights—right down to the lighted Christmas wreath on the front grill. *Don't let Amelia see that*, he thought to himself. *She'll want one of her own.* The annoyance he'd felt with such decorations had subsided lately, replaced by the first hints of a warm association as every tree, star or bulb reminded him of something from Amelia's house.

A black pickup pulled into the intersection behind the semi, Finn's senses coming to full alert as he noticed a familiar scrape on the passenger side. Boone had to have known what he'd done—didn't the guy have smarts enough fix the dent and remove the evidence? Furthermore, Lizzie had told Amelia she and Boone were going to that premarital workshop at their church tonight—what was he doing pulling out of town instead?

It wasn't really a clear decision—more like a suspicious hunch than anything else—that made Finn flick the turn signal the other direction and follow the truck outside of town. The process came back to him like an old habit—follow two or three cars back, stay unobtrusive, don't do anything to arouse suspicion. When Boone's truck pulled into an open field, Finn killed the lights on Amelia's car and watched from the far corner. Boone backed the truck up to a rotted old barn, walked inside for a few moments and then returned to restart the engine with its familiar loud growl. Seconds later the truck pulled away from the barn to reveal a livestock trailer now attached.

Nobody moves livestock at night, Finn realized, *unless they'd rather not be seen. Unless they aren't supposed to be moving livestock at all.*

When he saw movement in the trailer, he didn't need any further facts. No one kept cattle in a trailer in a run-down barn in the middle of nowhere unless they were *hiding* them. Finn twisted the ignition keys, sending the car into life to race down the road and cut off the gravel drive where Boone's truck was headed.

Finn got out of the car to stand in the truck's oncoming headlights, squinting as the glare blinded his eyes. The truck ground to a stop just in front of him and gunned its engine, a black metal predator rumbling in menace. The truck inched forward a foot or two with another gun of the engine, a clear signal to get out of the way.

Finn stood his ground. With the trailer fixed behind, the truck didn't have enough room to turn off the gravel road into the fields. He waited for the flash of panic to return, the bolt of fear that had run through him the first time he'd seen the truck. The scene replayed in his head, but without the pounding pulse of the earlier recurrence. Now Finn felt his chest fill with a lawman's cold, clear determination. "Get out of the truck, Boone," he shouted.

No answer came from the darkened windows of the cab.

Finn reached into his pocket and pulled out the silver star of a badge he'd retrieved from his dresser drawer back at the apartment. It glinted in the headlights as the low moan of anxious cattle rose up from the trailer. "I said get out of the truck, Boone." Just because Boone Lawton seemed like the kind of guy who'd try anything, Finn added, "And keep your hands where I can see them, if you please."

The forced calm with which Boone climbed out of the truck was almost comical. As if they'd met in the line at the grocery store. "Hey there, Finn. Whatcha doin' all the way out here?"

"I should ask you the same question. I thought you were at church tonight with Lizzie."

Boone tossed his head back toward the trailer, his shaggy hair falling into his eyes. "Last-minute job. You know, needing extra money for the wedding and all."

This guy really couldn't be smart enough to pull off all those rustling jobs, could he? Or was the dumb-ranch-hand persona all an act? "Really? Who'd need cattle moved out here? At this hour?"

Boone's laugh was high and tight. "Hey, look, man—I'm just doing my job here. I don't need you poking your nose into my business. Since when are you with the Rangers anyhow?"

Technically, Finn was on leave from the force, but Boone didn't need to know that. Nor did he need to know Finn was unarmed. The way Boone kept staring at the badge, the silver star was all the weapon Finn needed. He didn't bother answering Boone's question. "Where'd the cattle come from?"

"What's it to you?"

"Could be a lot to me, seeing as how so many things have gone missing in Little Horn lately. Seeing as how your truck has a scrape on the passenger-side door that feels highly familiar."

Boone sat back on one hip and stuck his hands into his back pockets. "I thought you don't remember nothing."

"How do you know what I remember?" Finn started walking around to the far side of the truck. "Could be I remember a lot of things. Could be I remember where this scrape came from." With a surprising, almost eerie calm, Finn ran his finger down the dent in the door.

Boone came around to stand in front of him, his hand protectively on the truck. "You came out of nowhere, man. I didn't even see you before it was too late. I didn't know you were hurt bad. I didn't even know who you were."

"I know the feeling," Finn said. "I didn't know who I was when I woke up, either."

Boone put his hands up. "Okay, that was weird. I mean, I never meant for all that to happen. I was just thinking with all this rustling going on, everybody would assume it was the bandit guy. He's hitting all the rich ranchers, so why not make a few bucks on the little guys while everyone's back is turned? So I took a few head of cattle once or twice and sold 'em out of town. Who'd miss it in all the fuss, right?"

He wasn't the Robin Hood rustler? That made a sad sort of sense.

"I'm sorry, okay? We can get past this, right?" Boone's words were speeding up as he paced on the gravel. "It's just you and me here, and we can just forget all this happened. Hey, I'll even put these cows back if that'll make you happy. No one else needs to know."

This guy really was a piece of work. Lizzie needed to learn what bad news Boone Lawton was, and fast. Amelia could help her little sister realize how broken engagements were a lot less messy than broken marriages. "Hand over the keys to the truck and get into this car with me."

That got Boone's attention. "Not on your life."

Finn opened the door and began climbing up into the truck cab to retrieve the keys, still dangling from the ignition.

Boone grabbed his arm. "Get out of my truck!"

Finn felt his still-healing shoulder burn with pain but twisted his arm out of Boone's grasp. With a speed and agility his body seemed to remember without thinking, Finn flipped in the truck seat and sent his bootheel hard onto the bridge of Boone's nose. Boone tipped back with a sickening crunch as his hands went up to the blood gushing from his nose. He staggered for a moment, letting out a string of curses from behind his seeping hands. It gave Finn just enough time to pull his own belt from his jeans and wrestle Boone's arms behind him as he shoved the young man up against his own truck.

"Fine," Finn said as he pulled the buckle tight around Boone's writsts and looped the leather around itself several times. "We'll take yours. I wouldn't want you to bleed all over Amelia's car anyhow." He found Boone's cell phone in the truck console and flipped it open. Sure enough, Lizzie's name was at the top of the Recent Calls list. He pulled up the number and held it to Boone's ear even as blood still streamed down the man's face. "Tell Lizzie to meet you at Amelia's in twenty minutes."

"No way." Boone spit blood out of his mouth. "You're crazy."

Finn reared up his elbow and poised it just in front of Boone's surely broken nose. "As a matter of fact, my brain's working just fine at the moment. Now talk."

Chapter Seventeen

Amelia pulled open the door to see Lizzie's panicked scowl. "What's happened?" she cried. "Why am I supposed to meet Boone here? Did you say something to him?"

"Your call was the first I'd heard of this," Amelia replied as Lizzie pushed past her. "I don't know anything more than you do."

Lizzie flung her coat over a living room chair and stalked back toward the kitchen. "I put on some coffee," Amelia called after her, hoping to soften her sister's prickly composure. Whatever was happening, it had the makings of a long night.

Gramps, ready for bed an hour ago, shuffled into the kitchen in his bathrobe. "Someone want to tell me what's going on here?"

"Ask her!" Lizzie barked, pointing at Amelia.

Amelia pulled in a deep breath and went to the

fridge to pull out coffee creamer. "Believe me, if I knew, I'd tell you. I don't think we'll know anything until Boone arrives."

"Boone? Why is Boone coming here?" Grandpa had never been a fan of late-night visitors, much less angry ones.

"He sounded upset. Like he was sick or something." Lizzie dumped three teaspoons of sugar into the coffee and stirred it vigorously. "Something's wrong."

"Well, that's clear enough," Grandpa huffed. "I'm going to have to go get dressed again. Beats me what's so important it can't wait till morning."

Amelia had entertained the same thought. "You don't have to stay up for this, Gramps." In fact, she rather envied his excuse to hide. This had the makings of a world-class drama, and she wasn't in the mood for it. The last thing she needed was Finn walking in on this explosion when she needed time alone with that man. *Lord, I want to believe You saw this coming, but I'm stumped but good.*

Just as she was filling her coffee cup, she saw the high, wide lights of Boone's truck pull into the driveway.

"He's here." Lizzie put down her cup and rushed to the door.

Amelia took a long drink and closed her eyes in a prayer for grace. Her eyes shot wide open when she heard Lizzie's scream. "Lord have mercy! Call 911!"

Amelia grabbed the phone and rushed to the hallway to see a bloody, angry Boone being thrust through her front door by none other than Finn. Boone's shirt was caked with blood and his eyes were practically swollen shut behind the bag of ice he held to his nose.

As Amelia started to dial, Finn held up his hand. "He doesn't need an ambulance. Lizzie can take him to the ER when we're through here if he still wants it, but I don't think I broke his nose."

Amelia practically dropped the phone. "You? *You* punched Boone in the nose?"

"Kicked," Boone corrected through what sounded like a very fat lip. "He kicked me in the head like a mule."

Lizzie alternated between fawning over Boone and shooting black looks at Finn. "Why did you hurt him like that?"

In seconds everyone was shouting at everyone else until Amelia banged the phone against the wall as loudly as she could. "Please! Let's get into the kitchen where Boone can sit down and we can make some sense of this." *If there is any sense to be made of this*, she thought as she pointed toward the kitchen A whimpering Lizzie, a brooding Boone and a completely unreadable Finn followed her directions.

Finn seemed the calmest of the bunch, so she started with him as she wet a dishcloth and handed it to Lizzie. "What on earth happened?" With Boone now slumped head back in one of the kitchen chairs, Lizzie began to wipe blood off of the man's streaked and swollen face.

"Did something happen at work, Pookie?" Lizzie sounded near tears and she replaced the ice bag.

"Boone wasn't at work." Finn's sharp, factual tone reminded Amelia that he was a Ranger.

"Of course he was," Lizzie countered, one hand on Boone's cheek as she glared over her shoulder at Finn.

"I came across his truck turning just outside of town on my way back from Austin. I followed him."

"You followed him?" Lizzie's words were more accusation than question. "Since when are you the police?"

Boone made a growling sound at that, and Amelia stepped in before the growl became a roar. "Finn is with the Texas Rangers, Lizzie." It didn't come close to explaining whatever was happening, but someone had to start somewhere. "What happened when you followed Boone?"

"So you *weren't* at work?" Lizzie's pity was in sudden danger of evaporating into annoyance.

"Well, I..." came Boone's voice from under the ice bag.

Lizzie pulled off the ice bag to scowl at Boone. "So you lied to me? You skipped out on premarital counseling by *lying* to me?"

The look in Finn's eyes told Amelia this was about to get much worse than a simple lovers' spat. She repeated her question as calmly as she could. "What did you find when you followed Boone?"

Finn picked up a dishrag from the stack Amelia had put on the kitchen table and began to wipe the blood off his own hands. "I found him hitching a trailer of stolen cattle up to his truck."

Lizzie pulled back in shock. "*You're* the Robin Hood Rustler?"

"No!" moaned Boone.

"No," said Finn.

"No?" Amelia and Lizzie said in shockingly perfect timing.

"I didn't do all that other stuff," Boone said, his battered nose distorting the words.

"But you did steal cattle?" Lizzie glared at her fiancé. "Rustling? Boone, how could you do such a thing?"

"Evidently Boone thought he could pull in a few extra dollars with some petty theft from some of the smaller ranches while everyone's attention was diverted by the crimes on the bigger outfits," Finn explained. "A poor copycat, I'm afraid."

And not a very smart one at that, Amelia thought. While she would have liked to say the revelation surprised her, it hadn't. Lizzie, on the other hand, was deflating with more heartbreak and disappointment by the second. Whatever other doubts Amelia had about the couple, two things were becoming quickly clear. One, that Lizzie had indeed loved Boone deeply; and two, that it didn't look as if their engagement would last the night. *Another Klondike engagement gone bust. We sure could use a dose of happiness soon, Lord.* The Christmas carol clock chimed the late hour with "Silent Night." *This night is anything but silent, and all is definitely not calm. Help me, Jesus, I don't know what to do.*

"Are you going to arrest him?" Lizzie's question to Finn was so weary and emotionless Amelia couldn't tell if Lizzie wanted Boone in custody or feared it.

"Technically, I'm on leave from the Rangers. I don't have the authority to arrest him."

Amelia very much wanted to know why Finn was on leave, but now didn't seem like a prudent time to ask.

"*Now* he tells me," Boone said from under his ice pack. Amelia found the young man awfully cocky for someone in so much trouble.

"I do have the authority to force you to come clean to your fiancée and her family. About everything."

Lizzie leaned back against the kitchen wall. "There's more?"

Finn leveled a chilly glare at Boone. "How many times have you stolen cattle from small ranchers, Boone?"

"Just a few."

Lizzie put her hands over her eyes, and Amelia reached out to touch her poor sister's shoulder. As bad as Rafe's skewed priorities were, finding out the man you loved was a criminal—and a seemingly unrepentant one at that—had to feel much worse.

"An actual number, if you don't mind," Finn pressed.

"Three. Well, four. The fourth one was just some equipment. I didn't keep none of it. I sold it to a guy I know the next town over. Really, it was for money for the wedding."

"And maybe a shiny new truck?" Lizzie had drawn the same conclusion Amelia had.

"I wanted the best for us, baby," Boone cooed, pulling the ice bag from his face to look at Lizzie and reach for her hand.

Lizzie kept her hand away from Boone's and straightened up off the wall. "The best for *us*, baby," she gave the endearment a knife's edge, "would have been to get a real job and show up at church like you promised." She held up her left hand. "The best thing for me is to end this right now." With that she worked the small ring off her finger and tossed it at him. "We're finished."

"Baby, Pookie…" Boone pleaded.

"Actually, you're not finished. Not quite yet. Lizzie and Amelia, I think you both need to hear what else Boone has to say."

Amelia couldn't think of anything that could be worse than what she'd just heard. She looked at Finn for any clue, but his face was hard and cold. "Tell them," he said to Boone. Amelia could practically hear Finn's teeth grinding behind the words. "Now," he growled when Boone hesitated.

"I…well, I didn't know it at the time, but… I'm the one who hit Finn."

Amelia felt the room spin as she sank into a chair.

"It was at night. He was in the road trying to stop me. I panicked and knocked him off the road. I didn't know he fell all the way down the ridge." Boone was slumping into his own chair now, looking as if it was finally dawning on him just how deep a whole he'd dug for himself.

She looked up at Finn, her face drawn tight with fear and confusion. She couldn't be more than four feet from him and yet she felt as if miles stretched between them. "How is that possible?"

"It came back to me when I saw the dent in Boone's truck at dinner last night. I was driving to a family cabin north of here where I had planned to spend December. I got out of the car by the pine woods to pick up some firewood when I came up on Boone moving that same trailer with a different set of cattle. Given the late hour and the fact that there was no ranch anywhere nearby, I was sure he was rustling. I tried to stop him, and that's when he ran me off the road. I recognized the truck and the black ski mask I found in Boone's toolbox."

"I mean it," Boone insisted. "I didn't know I'd hurt you bad. I just thought I scared you and you were hiding."

"Of course you didn't know," Finn replied, barely keeping his rising anger in check. "You drove off. Or at least you must have. How would I know what you did, seeing as I was lying unconscious at the bottom of the ridge?" he shouted.

"Boone, you could have killed him!" Amelia cried. "You broke his ribs. You gave him that huge cut and his concussion. You gave him the amnesia!"

"Get out of my granddaughter's house right now." Gramps's voice came from behind Finn with surprising authority. No one had realized

Gramps had entered the room. "And if your next stop isn't the police station to turn yourself in, I'll call them myself to come find you wherever you are."

Boone was at least smart enough to sense the very real threat in Gramps's voice. Within a minute of Finn tossing him the keys, Boone was out the door and into his truck. If he had any sense at all—which Amelia would question—he was headed toward the police station. Would turning himself in buy Boone any mercy? Given all the recent thefts, Amelia doubted Lucy would go lightly on him.

The room was silent for a minute as the roar of Boone's engine gunned and left the driveway. Then, as they all stared through the window at the fading red lights, Lizzie began to cry. In all her astonishment over Boone's crimes, Amelia had forgotten that her sister's heart had just been broken.

Gramps hadn't. The old man opened his arms to his granddaughter. "There, now, Lizzie girl." Compassion filled his soft voice. "You cry all you want. You've had a whole heap of hurt tonight. Why don't you come sit with me on the den couch and we'll fall asleep together like when you were little." The old man looked at Amelia over Lizzie's head. "I think these two have a few more things to talk out anyhow."

As Amelia watched them leave, the weight of the evening pressed down on her. Finn looked exhausted. He moved as if in pain, and his eyes squinted as if the kitchen light gave him a headache. His gazed searched around the room as if he couldn't figure out what to say next. "I never wanted any of this to happen."

"You went to your place…your *home* in Austin." She stumbled over the word and they both knew why.

"I did. I had to."

Amelia mustered up the courage to ask, "And what did you find?"

Finn rubbed his hands along the back of his neck, reaching for words. "It's empty. I mean there's furniture there, things that belong to me, but…" He shrugged. "It's…empty. It's like there's nothing there, even though there is."

She had to ask him. "Tell me what you haven't told me. All of it. Please."

"You mean Belinda." Finn's eyes told her he was fully aware what those words did to her.

"Belinda," she repeated, folding her hands together on the table. "Is that her name?"

"Yes, that was her name. Belinda was my wife."

Amelia looked up from her hands. "Was?"

He swallowed hard. "She was killed in a car

accident last Christmas. Along with our baby daughter."

Amelia shut her eyes, reeling from the weight of that declaration. She'd imagined a million things, but none as awful as that. "Oh, Finn. That's awful. What a terrible time for an accident."

Finn looked as if he were barely hanging on to his composure. His face was filled with pain, his fingers fisted tight against his palms and the muscles in his arms tensed. "It wasn't an accident. They were killed."

What had been sad and cruel became devastating. Amelia felt her heart twist and tears burn in her eyes for all this man had lost.

"The partner of a man I put in jail cut the brake lines on Belinda's car. He made sure my family would die." He swallowed again, and she could see him struggle to keep the grief from consuming him. "Dr. Searle showed me the police file that day you found me in the park." He looked up at her, his eyes so forlorn that Amelia let her own tears come. "I couldn't even remember them when I saw the photos. How is that fair?" he agonized. "How is that right?"

"Oh, Finn. I can't imagine…"

"I couldn't tell anyone—wouldn't speak their names, even to you—until I felt the grief I ought to have felt. Until I mourned them. Felt their loss the way I was supposed to, not by some cheat of a lost memory."

"But you did. You remembered them."

"This afternoon I sat at my kitchen table in Austin and it came back. Like breaking open a box or…or switching a light on in a dark room." He swallowed hard, fighting for control. "And I remembered them. Remembered being with them. And then I remembered what it was like to be without them. I remembered their funerals and what it was like to pack up those tiny pink pajamas and…" He put his hands up over his eyes, choked into silence.

Finn gave a groan and pushed up out of the chair. "I thought I wanted to remember," he told Amelia as he paced the kitchen. "I thought I owed them that much. They deserve to be remembered." He turned to look at her. "Only there's so much pain. It wasn't there when I didn't remember. But it's back. I was so sure nothing could be worse than not remembering—" he ran his hands through his hair with a heartbreaking air of desperation "—but it's *so much worse*. I wish I didn't remember—how terrible is that? What kind of man wishes he didn't remember his family?"

She was openly crying now, not even bothering to stop the flow of tears. "Oh, Finn. Who could blame God for wanting to spare you so much pain even for a little while?"

She wasn't sure if it was anger or hopelessness that flashed through is eyes. "God didn't do this to me. Boone Lawton did. It was just dumb luck that you were the one who found me." He leaned back against the counter farthest from her, wrapping his hands around his chest as if he he might explode from the onslaught of pain. "I almost wish you hadn't found me at all."

That pushed her up out of her chair. "Don't say that. You know it wasn't luck—there is no luck, Finn, only God's purposes we can't always see. I don't believe I found you for no reason and neither do you."

He shook his head. "I'm alone, Amelia. I just forgot it for a while, but it doesn't change what's true." She hated that he turned away from her. "I can't go back to being the person I was when I was here, when I couldn't remember."

"Don't leave now," she pleaded, wiping her wet cheeks with one hand. "I don't want you to go. I don't know how we sort through this but I know I don't want you to leave." She grabbed his shoulder and tried to turn him toward her even though he resisted. "How could you possibly spend Christmas alone with all you've been through?"

"That's exactly what I was planning to do. That's where I was headed that night, up to a cabin where I could spend Christmas alone.

Where I wouldn't have to try and be a human being, where I could just..." Finn's hands flailed in the air. "I don't even know. Maybe merely survive, come out the other side of it still upright and breathing. Only I'm not even sure that's possible. It doesn't feel like it now."

"You can't go," she repeated.

"I can. I have to. Just let me walk out of your life, okay?"

"No, you can't." She sniffed, and it took him a moment to realize she was half laughing, half crying. "I mean, you can't. There's no car." He'd forgotten he'd come in Boone's truck. Near as Amelia could tell, her car was still outside of town by that barn.

He stared at her, stunned. "I can call a cab."

"Don't you dare," she scolded, emboldened by everything she'd just heard and even admitted to herself. "We need to talk. I don't want you to leave like this." After a long moment, she dared to add, "I don't want you to leave at all."

Finn squeezed his eyes shut. "You say you don't want me to leave. I didn't want to leave. I still don't. But that can't matter." He opened his eyes again, his gaze pleading. "None of that changes that I'm still a Ranger. The people I love were killed because of it. This wasn't just a missed dinner or a broken engagement—this was murder. *Murder*, Amelia. That's not a life you want. I don't have anything you want."

Amelia stood her ground in front of him. "I believe God led me to that forest to find you. I don't know if I saved your life—maybe we'll never know that—but I believe—" she put her hand to her heart rather than reach out to touch his "—I believe in my heart I was sent to help you. Doesn't that count for anything?"

Finn turned to look out the window. She saw his hands grip the counter. "It counts for everything," he said, still not turning back toward her. "I'll never be able to thank you enough for that."

"Then thank me by not leaving. At least not in the middle of the night like this. Wait until morning, that's all I ask. Please."

She knew the moment her last plea pulled all the resistance from him. His shoulders sank and he exhaled. She'd stand there and argue with him until he gave in. She would not let him walk out the door and be swallowed by the cold night. As if he knew he could be the last straw, Bug walked into the room and looked up at Finn with pitiful, bulging eyes.

Gramps appeared in the doorway. "Three to one—you're outnumbered." He hobbled over to Finn and put an arm on his shoulder. "Nothin' good'll happen if you head out now. Best to see what the morning brings, son. No one will stop you if you need to go then."

Finn nodded, caught Amelia's eyes for a long moment and then turned toward the stairs. She watched him climb the steps, her heart twisting further when Bug followed him.

Chapter Eighteen

Amelia startled awake at the sound Bug's barking and a knock on her front door. She tossed the blanket from her lap, surprised to see the sun coming through the living room windows as she headed for the door.

"I hear you had quite a night over here," Lucy said. "Boone Lawton turned himself in for stealing cattle and for hit-and-run." The sheriff raised an eyebrow that was half official business, half friendly concern. "You want to tell me the rest of the story?"

Amelia wasn't even sure she knew what the rest of the story was. "I'm surprised I dozed off. I was sure I'd be up all night praying."

Lucy stepped inside when Amelia opened the door farther, then managed a chuckle as she looked up to see Bug run up the stairs to stare at Finn's closed door. "I still can't believe it."

Amelia stared at the door. "I can't believe Bug slept up there with Finn most of the night."

"So Finn is still here?" Lucy shucked off her jacket. "Boone made it sound like Finn was headed back to Austin."

"I think he would have tried walking all the way back, but Gramps and I talked him in to waiting for daylight." Amelia hesitated before adding, "He told me everything, Lucy. It's simply awful." As Amelia started the coffeepot, she told Lucy what Finn had shared about his late family and the life he had in Austin. "He's been through so much it's a wonder he's still standing. It feels like a terrible thing to say, but I can't help wondering if God sent the amnesia just to give him a chance to breathe and heal."

Lucy sat down at the table. "That's too much for any man to carry alone."

Amelia sat down at the table as the coffeepot gurgled to life. "He talks as if being a Ranger dooms everyone who is close to him. Rafe never spoke like that. I knew there were risks, but…"

"Makes it easy to see why the Rangers kept everything out of the papers. A story like that is hard to swallow, even for me." Lucy nodded toward the staircase. "I need to talk to him, to see if he wants to press charges against Boone."

Amelia followed her friend's gaze. "Well, that's one good reason he stayed, I suppose." She'd stared up the staircase at that closed door for hours last night, praying that God would sort this whole thing out. "Honestly, I don't know what's good or bad anymore." She returned her gaze to Lucy. "I prayed all night for God to send some kind of comfort to Finn because I didn't know what else to do to help him."

"The unsinkable Amelia Klondike not knowing how to help? That's a first." Lucy's words were teasing, but her eyes held a compassion for Amelia's tumult.

"I can't change his past. I can't help him cope with what he remembers. And he's right—I can't change that he's a Ranger." Amelia ran her hands through her hair, suddenly realizing she must look a fright after having spent the night fitfully dozing in a recliner. "Look at me—I can't even sleep this is such a mess." The Christmas carol clock chimed 7:00 a.m.—"Joy to the World." "Some joyful Christmas. The League party is at six and all I feel like doing is crawling under a rock to hide."

Lucy made her way to the coffeemaker. "Now I know you're really a mess. If you can't muster up some holiday spirit, the rest of us are in trouble." As she poured two cups of the steaming brew, the radio at her belt gave a beep. "Speaking of trouble…" Lucy pressed the button on the device. "What is it, Ed?"

"Another robbery, boss. The Thompson ranch. They brought a dozen new head of cattle onto the place two days ago and woke up this morning to find four of 'em gone."

"The ones Boone took?" Amelia asked.

"I wish it were that easy," Lucy said. "We returned those to the Baker place last night. I would have brought your car back from the scene except Finn had the keys." She pressed the button on the radio again after she set the cups down. "Okay Ed. I'm taking a statement from Finn Brannigan right now, so I'll be there as soon as I can."

"There's more, boss," Ed said from the radio. "The Derrings woke up to five new head of cattle and a bunch of new farm equipment. And their foster kids got presents, too."

Lucy raised an eyebrow. "Timmy Johnson and Maddy Coles got presents?"

"Some new winter coats and—hang on, let me find my notes here—some books, new backpacks and two new iPods. Looks like our Robin Hood even knew red was Maddy's favorite color."

Lucy shook her head. "Thanks, Ed. See you soon." She looked at Amelia. "Who'd know all that? Maddy's best friend was Betsy McKay, but she's been gone for months. This just gets stranger every day."

"Well," Amelia admitted, "at least now we can be sure our Robin Hood isn't Boone." She sighed.

"I still can't believe he stole cattle after everything else that's been going on. And he lied to Lizzie." She sighed, breathing in the comforting scent of freshly brewed coffee. "Another broken engagement. Poor Lizzie, she's heartbroken."

Lucy leaned in. "And is she the only one?"

What was the state of her heart at the moment? "I don't know. I thought when I got an explanation from Finn that it would settle everything, but it's settled nothing. It's made everything worse, I think." Amelia sipped her coffee, feeling it soothe the aches of her restless night. "Gramps told me to ask him how he felt about me, that it was the most important question, but we never got to that. We got tangled up in the whole mess of what happened to him."

"And do you still care about him? Now that you know all of it?"

Amelia looked at her friend, tears threatening. "I think I care about him more. And that's worse, because I need to care about him less. I need to shut it off, I need to not care because it won't work. It can't work." She lost the battle to the tears, feeling them slide down her cheeks as her throat tightened up. "Finn is right—no matter how important I can be to him, that just makes me a bigger target for anyone who wants to hurt him. I can't go through that, and he surely can't."

Lucy's face hardened a bit, and Amelia recognized that wasn't a fair thing to say to Lucy. As sheriff, Lucy faced the same risks as a Ranger or anyone in law enforcement—any firefighter or soldier or prosecutor, for that matter—but if she didn't speak the words, she thought the sorrow would rise up and swallow her whole. "I'm sorry," she said as she dabbed her eyes on one of the napkins sitting at the table. "That wasn't fair."

"It's true," Lucy said with resignation in her voice. "To love someone in our field means to risk a lot." She reached for Amelia's hand. "But I know plenty of Rangers who died as old, happily married men. They lived long lives proud of what they did and the people they protected. That's a chance your parents never got. Seems to me, it's a risk to love anyone."

Amelia sniffed and dabbed her eyes again. "That sounds like something Gramps would say."

"He'd be right. He'd also tell you it's better to have loved and lost than never to have loved at all."

Amelia managed a laugh. "That wasn't Gramps, that was Tennyson." Too many people had quoted the poet to her after her broken engagement.

"Then they'd both be right." Lucy squared her shoulders. "Look, I'm not going to tell you what to do—you have to work that out for yourself. But if he came straight with you and told you everything and you still love him, then maybe it's worth fighting for."

"I didn't say I loved him."

Lucy raised an eyebrow. "You didn't need to. Don't ever try cards or crime, Amelia—you don't have the face to pull it off. Whatever you're thinking or feeling shows clear as day." She drained her coffee and looked at the bright sunlight now shining in the kitchen window. "And the day is getting away from me already. I need you to go wake Finn so I can get this over with."

"Sure." Amelia didn't feel ready as she climbed the stairs to knock on Finn's door, but really, would she ever feel ready to face all this tumult?

"Finn?" Bug, who had followed her up the stairs, put his paw on the door as if to knock himself. "You need to wake up and talk to Sheriff Lucy about last night."

When no reply came, she knocked again, jealous of the obvious deep sleep he'd gotten when she felt wrung out. "Finn?"

When no answer came again, she pushed the door open. An empty room greeted her, with a made bed, his things gone and a sheet of paper laid carefully on the pillow.

Finn was gone.

It was cold for Texas in December. Finn was glad he'd brought the jacket from his apartment, muddy and bloody as it had gotten during his scuffle with Boone and the livestock trailer. He looked down at the bloodstain on his sleeve and wondered if he looked so bedraggled that someone would turn him over to the sheriff before giving him a ride. Chilly as it was, the slow pour of sunshine into the sky and the space of the open road before him felt good. Maybe the walk would clear his head. After all, it wasn't that far to Maggie's Coffee Shop. A big cup of coffee, a call to a cab and Finn could put Little Horn behind him.

Trouble was, the pink of the early-morning sky reminded Finn of Amelia's cheeks as she smiled over her cupcakes that night at the food-truck court. And the bluer the sky turned, the more it looked like her eyes. He wanted to think he was walking away from Amelia, but instead she was turning up everywhere, all around him.

I'm too broken to love her. The thought sent a stronger chill down his back than any dawn breeze swirling dust down the road. Amelia deserved someone who matched her zest for life, someone who would treat her like the extraordinary treasure she was. It burned in his chest that he could see exactly what she needed—and see just as clearly that he was not the man to give it to her.

I love her anyway. It ought to have been the kind of sentiment shouted in happiness, but for

Finn it was uttered in defeat. All the sensibility in the world, all the reasons why he wouldn't bring her into the disaster that had become his life, didn't change what he felt for her. In fact, it was the care he felt for her that sent his feet down this road and away from her. To love her from outside of her life would be the kindest thing he could do for Amelia. *I'm letting her go, Lord, to someone she deserves.*

It surprised Finn how easily the prayer came. He felt a tiny shred less alone as he walked down the road, watching the sun push the darkness out of the sky. Luther was right—it was easier to see things in the daylight. And wasn't it Luther who'd said *if you still need to go...*

Forgive me for not saying goodbye to her, he prayed. *I took the coward's way out. But if You really do know everything, You know how Amelia is. I'd never stand a chance against those eyes.*

Then, in a surprising surge of resignation, Finn added, *Thanks for the time I had with her. Thanks for sending her to me. I'll bear what I have now and try not to complain.* Thinking that sounded a bit high-and-mighty for someone who hadn't prayed since Sunday school, Finn opted for honesty. This was God, after all; it wasn't as if a man could pull anything over on the Almighty. *But it hurts. Bad.*

Make friends with the pain. Invite it in—it's

coming in anyway. It took Finn a half mile of walking to figure out where that voice in his head came from. Lieutenant Keeland, his field superior on the force, had said it to him the day before Belinda and Annie's funeral. Keeland had known his share of loss in life—his wife had left him thanks to the demands of the force—so he spoke from experience. Finn could pull Keeland's face up clearly in his memory now. He could also pull up the day of Keeland's own funeral, just two months after his retirement this past April. Stan Keeland died alone. Rafe had been right to recognize what the Ranger life did to a family. If Finn had been smart enough to see that, Belinda might still be alive today.

But then Annie would never have come to be. Annie was tiny and bubbly and wonderful. The light of Finn's life. He'd gone overboard and bought so many Christmas presents for the little girl, and she wasn't even old enough to hold a doll. He'd thrown everything away—all the presents for Belinda and Annie—unable to have them near and unwilling to return anything.

Keep walking, Finn told himself. *Every step you take away from Amelia gives her a better shot at happiness. She's better off without you— even she'll come to admit that soon enough.*

Finn was almost grateful for the numbness chilling his bones as he pushed through the doors at Maggie's Coffee Shop in town. They'd just opened, and the place was relatively empty—the ranchers were still finishing up their chores. An hour from now, the place would be packed.

An hour from now, he'd be on his way to Austin.

"What'll it be?" the friendly waitress asked.

"Coffee, to go. Black."

"No danish to go with that, cowboy?" She had a sweet smile. He was glad she didn't know his name nor ask it. It was best for everyone if Finn slipped out of town unnoticed.

"Nope. Just the coffee."

The waitress nodded toward Finn's bag. "Headed home for the holidays?"

"Yeah, you could say that." He had no "home" in that sense, only a space he occupied. A home looked like Amelia's house, not like his.

"Well, then, Merry Christmas to you. Coffee's on the house."

Finn dug into his pockets, not wanting to be anyone's charity. "No, really, I'll pay." He'd even tip big, just to put a sparkle in her holiday. Someone ought to be happy this time of year, even if it couldn't be him. *It won't be Amelia, either,* his conscience reminded him. That couldn't be helped, and by next Christmas she'd thank him, another bad relationship choice put behind her like Rafe.

"You're up early."

Finn turned to see Carson Thorn.

"Brannigan, is that it?" The man held out a friendly hand. "Carson Thorn. I don't expect you to remember my name, given your condition and all."

My condition. Thorn's words were meant to put him at ease, but they sunk into Finn's gut and weighted him down. "No, I remember. I'm better now, thanks." Now, there was an overstatement. "Well enough to head home." The claim felt false and hollow.

"I'm sure your kin will be happy to have you back after everything. Luther tells me you've been great company at the house, and Lucy tells me even that little dog took a shine to you."

Poor guy, he couldn't know the weight of what he was saying. "The Klondikes have been more than kind to me, that's for sure."

"Well, you know you're always welcome back for a visit. We haven't had a Ranger in town since Rafe—not that we've needed any more excitement lately. Little Horn's had a tough, crazy season. I'll be glad to put it behind us for a while at the League Christmas party tonight. It's a shame you won't be joining us."

The waitress set the foam cup of coffee down in front of Finn. "Christmas isn't really my thing anyhow."

"What? You mean Amelia's full-out Christmas cheer isn't infectious? That house always looks like the holiday section of a department store to me. Ruby told me she has a clock that..."

"...that chimes Christmas carols, yeah, she does." Suddenly Finn felt surrounded by details that kept pointing back to Amelia, as if all of Little Horn were latching on to him, resisting letting him leave. "I gotta go. My cab will be here any minute."

"Cab? Where you headed?"

"Austin."

"No kidding? Cancel that cab. I'm on my way into Austin, as well. I'll be happy to drive you. I need a little company this early in the morning anyhow."

"No, really, I..."

"Nonsense. That'd cost you a fortune anyway. And the bus is usually overrun with college kids, so you definitely don't want that." Carson put his check on the counter with a ten-dollar bill and pulled out his keys. "Ride with me. I never did hear your whole dramatic story—you can tell me on the way."

Chapter Nineteen

Finn tried steady his breathing and read Carson's face as he drove. He couldn't tell if the man's expression was shock, sympathy or suspicion. Maybe all three. "I hadn't really planned to unload all of that on you." Somehow the entire story leading up to his current retreat back home—and that was how he'd begun to think of it; a retreat—poured out of him when Carson had asked the reason for his Austin trip. Maybe it was the sleepless night that rendered Finn powerless to hold it in, and the whole thing now hung between them. The truck cab felt thick and close, as if the darkness of his story won out over the now-risen sun. "You probably wish I really had gotten into that cab, huh?" He tried to laugh, but it came out like a low whimper. Telling the whole disaster to a mere acquaintance like Carson Thorn made Finn feel as if someone had pried all his armor loose.

Carson ran a hand across his chin just before he took the Austin exit. "I had no idea. I knew you'd lost your memory, but I didn't realize all that led up to it. And Boone? Wow. I thought my life had done a good job of tangling into knots this fall, but yours takes the prize. It's a blessing Amelia found you when she did."

"Yeah." Finn tried to keep his voice neutral. "Amelia."

Carson shot him a look. "Want to explain that?"

Finn looked out the window, wishing his heart wasn't sinking with every mile that brought him closer to Austin. "That what?"

Carson grunted. "I'm no shrink, but even I can hear what's going on in the way you say her name."

He had to keep pulling his hand from the door handle. The urge to escape the truck—and the now-exposed truth—itched under his rib cage. "Amelia's a nice lady."

Carson pulled up at a red light at the bottom of the exit ramp. "Really? After all you just spilled to me you're gonna go with 'She's a nice lady'?"

Finn knew he was lost. After so many weeks of not knowing things or keeping roaring emotions in check, now every truth scrambled to get out. He evaded anyway. "She's a *really* nice lady?"

Carson's resulting glare said everything his silence did not.

An excruciating pause let Finn know he wouldn't be allowed out of the truck without further explanation. Maybe it would be better to talk it through with someone who wasn't Luther or Amelia. Finn removed his hand from the door handle yet again, beginning with the only fact that mattered. "I'd only hurt her."

Carson thought for a moment. "You know that for sure?"

Didn't Thorn hear any of what Finn just said? "How can it end any other way?"

"Maybe. Seems to me Amelia's made of tough stuff. She knows for herself what could hurt her. That whole business with Rafe spelled that out clearly enough."

"All the more reason not to let her in for another round of misery." *Misery.* The word had begun to stick to him, a pallor he'd never shake off. The term *a miserable existence* was taking on a personal meaning. This wasn't just "inviting the pain in," this was being consumed by it.

"Have you bothered to ask her?"

Finn put his hands over his eyes for a moment, finding the cheery sunshine blinding. *Had* he asked? He and Amelia had talked about everything long and hard, but did he ever come right out and ask her if she was willing to make a go of things between them? What woman in her right mind would even consider it?

"Or did you just decide yourself, and that's why you were heading out of town before dawn?"

Carson called his bluff. "I definitely should have taken that cab."

"No, I think it's a good thing you didn't." Carson shook his head. "I'm not blaming you for evasive maneuvers—Amelia's a one-woman army when she sets her mind to something."

Finn ran his hands through his hair. He'd become unbearably fidgety, and it had little to do with the coffee. "So everyone says. Believe me, I don't need convincing."

They came to another stoplight, and Carson turned to Finn. "Look, Brannigan, I won't pretend to know what it's like to lose an entire family way too soon. Everyone sees rough patches, but nothing I've been through ranks with the kind of loss you've had. It sounds unbearable. The worst kind of grief."

It was almost a relief to have Carson call his situation for the avalanche of pain that it was. Lots of people were quick to give "chin up" and "time will heal" platitudes that made him want to hit things and yell *It's awful and there's nothing anyone can do about it!*

"Only I'm not so sure it's a reason to cut

yourself off from someone as good as Amelia," Carson continued.

"It's not?" Finn sure thought it was.

"She's known a lot of loss, too. And her fair share of heartbreak. Still, she's held on to life in a way most of us couldn't. She has this ability to keep going we all admire. And hearts just don't come bigger or stronger than Amelia Klondike's. You really want to walk away from what could be the best thing to ever happen to you just because you're worried she can't handle the risk?"

Finn yearned to stomp out the irrational ember of hope Thorn's words ignited in his chest. "It's not that simple, Thorn."

"I think it is. You either move forward or back. Before Ruby came back to town, I thought I was moving forward, but I really wasn't." On the drive, Carson had shared the story of how his fiancée, Ruby, had been pushed from his life but had returned. Sure, they'd worked through their share of hurts, but just because Carson got his happy ending didn't mean everyone else got theirs. "I may be the last guy on earth qualified to give relationship advice," Carson went on, "but you're looking at a guy who almost let a good thing go. I'd hate to see you make that mistake."

When Finn didn't answer, Carson shot him another look. "You know Amelia would say it wasn't an accident she was the one to find you. Amelia believes God puts people in her path to help."

That had been the hardest part. Half of him was ready, eager to believe God had sent him Amelia. She seemed to be the antidote to so many of the poisons in his life. Around her, Finn could almost believe that happiness wouldn't always be out of reach. Still, he couldn't bring himself to be that selfish. To take what she gave, and give her only risk and harm in return? No, he had to protect Amelia from what her giant, optimistic heart refused to accept. "She's got way more faith than I have. Maybe more than I'll ever have."

The light changed and Carson kept driving. "So you figure you have to play the noble, sacrificing guy and save her from herself. I get it. Only that means you've decided you know better than God. You're saying that Him putting you and Amelia together was a mistake." Carson sighed. "Take it from me, that's a mighty dangerous way to think."

Finn didn't really care for a lecture this morning. "You think I should just pretend the facts don't matter? Hope my past stays forgotten?"

"I'm not saying that at all."

Finn's hand crept back onto the door handle. Even if it was miles to his apartment he could still pull the door open and bail out. "So what are you saying, Thorn?"

Carson turned a corner and pulled the truck to a stop. "I'm saying that I can't tell you what to do. But you can't tell Amelia what to do, either. But you've done that by leaving." He reached into his jacket pocket and pulled out a card. "My meeting is done at 3:00, and I'm driving back to Little Horn. I'd rather not make the drive alone. I'd rather bring you back to Little Horn, at least until you can get all this worked out."

Finn took the card. "I doubt I'll change my mind." He grabbed his bag from the back of the cab, thinking even if he had to walk clear across Travis County it would be easier than staying and listening to Carson Thorn chip away at his resolve.

"Your choice. But just remember one thing."

"What?" Finn opened the door.

"I'm with Amelia on this one. I don't think it's any accident that I was at Maggie's this morning on my way into Austin." Carson put a hand on Finn's arm as he was getting out of the truck. "God's handing you a rope, Finn. Grab it."

Amelia pulled on the bright red sweater that she always wore to the League Christmas party. *Christmas is still on its way. The Christ child still comes when my heart is broken. You came for broken hearts anyway, Jesus. Heal mine, even if only for tonight. I'm not the only one in Little Horn who needs Your joy.*

She thought again about the back office at the League headquarters, full to bursting with toys and gifts for so many in Little Horn. Happy faces and squeals of delight would do her good tonight.

"Pull yourself together, girl." Amelia addressed her reflection as she put on a pair of holly earrings. "Little Horn needs Christmas this year more than ever, and it's your job to make it happen."

As she reached for the wreath pin to fix to her sweater, her eye landed on the folded paper tucked against her mirror—the letter Finn had left. *Don't read it again*, she told herself even as she reached for it.

I can't stay, it said in Finn's bold hand. Of course he was the kind of man who wrote in all capital letters—he was intense about everything. *You've done so much for me. You made my escape from those memories something I'll always remember. It's why you deserve someone else. Have a wonderful life, Amelia.*

Have a wonderful life. Was there any more permanent way to say goodbye? If he wrote *Don't come looking for me*, he couldn't have been more clear. The split with Rafe had always felt like her own decision, even though his actions drove her to it. It felt as if Finn had ripped himself out of her life.

She knew why he had skipped the goodbye; she would have done anything to convince him to stay. She would have made him stay, somehow. Staying here in the first place, Christmas shopping, "stocking," she'd continually talked him into things he didn't want because she thought they were good for him. *I always think I know how to help everybody, don't I?*

Finn knew he wasn't yet strong enough to resist her relentless persuasion. That only made it worse, because it told her how much he truly did care. *Why can't it be enough, Lord? Why can't love be enough? What's the point of so many obstacles when the world is hard enough as it is?*

Amelia pulled in a deep breath, gave one last fix to her hair and walked out into the hallway. As she passed the stairs, she saw Bug lying at the top—his new favorite place to lay—staring at the door to Finn's room. Only it wasn't Finn's room anymore, was it? How was it she could feel that man all over this house when he'd been here less than a month?

"I know, pal," she said as Bug wobbled down the stairs to meet her. "I miss him, too."

Gramps came out of his room, handsome in the dark green sweater and maroon bow tie that was his Christmas party attire. His eyes told her he'd heard what she said. "Sometimes, all you get to do is plant the seed. God gives the harvest to someone else." He was talking about restoring Finn to faith, but he was talking about her heart, as well. "Some things even you can't fix. Finn has to heal on his own—if he heals at all."

"I hate not knowing where he is or if he's okay."

Gramps walked over and took her hand. "Silly. You know exactly where he is. He's in God's hands. Now it's your job to leave him there."

The threat of tears burned behind Amelia's eyes, and she pasted a teasing frown on her face. "Stop being so wise."

He pulled her into a hug for a few seconds. "I think a party is exactly what we need. Who's playing Santa this year?"

Gramps had taken the role of League Santa for years before the toll of squirming, sugar-hyped children became to much for his aging body. Since his "retirement," no consistent candidate had risen up to take his place. Every year Amelia had to wage an arm-twisting campaign to get someone to put on the red suit. Why it should be so hard to convince any of Little Horn's portlier ranchers to do something so fun was beyond her. "This year I've hit the bottom of the barrel, Gramps."

"Who?"

"Byron."

Gramps had every right to look astounded. "Byron McKay? He'd make a better Scrooge. What about Carson?"

As if she hadn't gone through the League rolls twice already, considering every other option. "And burst young Brandon's bubble when he recognizes his uncle under that white beard? I couldn't do that to a six-year-old. Besides, Carson's far too fit and trim to play Santa."

Gramps drew a breath to name another candidate, but Amelia stopped him. "And Doc Grainger's on call tonight—we can't very well have Santa's beeper going off and sending him rushing before presents get handed out, can we?"

"But *Byron*?"

"The suit's too big for anyone else, even if we pad it." She was ashamed to tell Gramps she'd found a smaller suit on sale and had every hope of convincing Finn to play Santa this year. It seemed like such a foolish idea to her now, and she couldn't find the energy to go convince someone else. "I had to promise the moon to get Byron to do it. Guess who's in charge of cleaning the League office for the next year?"

"Cleaning? You?"

She sighed. "I'll hire a couple of students from the high school and pay them out of my own pocket. Kids always need jobs anyways."

Gramps headed for the hall closet to fetch his

coat. "You would have been better off instituting a Mrs. Claus this year."

"No child wants to get his presents from Mrs. Claus. Honestly, even if I could find the costume, I think that would be worse than having no Santa at all."

"I don't know," Gramps muttered. "This is Byron we're talking about."

"Well—" Amelia helped Gramps with his buttons "—we'll just have to pray hard that Byron is struck by a sudden and whopping case of holiday cheer."

Gramps snorted. "Now, that would qualify as a Christmas surprise in my book." He stopped for a moment before heading toward the garage door. "You gonna be okay?"

"You know me." She applied a bright smile. "Unsinkable Amelia Klondike." A tiny crack in her heart reminded her that Finn had called her that, as well. Maybe not so tiny a crack. Maybe a wide, gaping hole. She adjusted Gramps's bow tie one more time. "Always Here to Help." In truth, there probably wasn't a better thing for her to be doing right now than bringing happiness to someone who needed it. She just wondered if that trusted antidote to her own pain would be enough to fill the hole left by Finn Brannigan.

Gramps caught her hand. "He hasn't fallen off the face of the earth, Amelia. Just gone away to heal. Either he'll come back healed, or he won't. I'm not saying you can't pray all you want about it, but I am saying this is something where you don't get to help."

As usual, Gramps hit the problem right on the head—and where it hurt the most. "Do *you* hope he'll come back, Gramps?"

Her grandfather's lips pursed in thought. "I think he could be a fine man if he made peace with all that's happened to him." He looked up at Amelia. There had been at time when he was taller than her, but age had stooped his shoulders even though it had never robbed the twinkle from his eye. "Do *you* want him to come back? After all, he's a Ranger. You know what all that means."

"I do. Only I've been thinking—what bothered me most about Rafe wasn't the risk, it was where I fit in his life. The badge always came first with Rafe, and always would. There's risk in every walk of life—look at poor Ben Stillwater still in a coma from riding across a pasture like dozens of ranchers do every day."

"And Finn?"

"I think he knows better than most men to treasure the people in his life. It's why he's not letting anyone close—they'd become precious to him." The words caught thick in her throat.

Gramps pushed the button that raised the garage doors. "Trouble is, we don't always get to choose when and how folks become precious to us."

She didn't mean for the unkind thought to slip out, but it did. "Rafe chose." Even though she'd made the decision to end it, and never regretted that choice, the whole business still stung of rejection. All the hindsight in the world didn't change that Rafe had chosen the badge over her.

Gramps turned to look at her. "You could say that. And it's sad—for you and for him. A man who makes those choices doesn't know what's precious in the first place." He touched Amelia's cheek. "You're precious to me, darlin.' And precious to God. And God willing, you'll be precious to the right man when he comes along."

Amelia never stopped believing that. She just feared the right man *had* come…and gone.

Chapter Twenty

Carson Thorn caught up with Amelia at the punch bowl. "Can I speak with you for a minute?"

Had he stopped in his office and seen the pile of gifts she'd stowed there when he said he'd be out for the day? "I only went a smidgen over budget, Carson, and I'll cover it out of my own pocket. After all, what's money for if not to spend on kids at Christmas?" In fact, Amelia had gone *way* over budget, channeling all her energies into present shopping. "You going to tell me you didn't go all out for that nephew of yours this year?"

Carson smiled. "Maybe, but this is about something else." He walked to his office and shut the door behind them. It was hard to do—the room was piled high with boxes and bags. He nodded toward the two Santa suits. Amelia had forgotten they both were here. Why didn't she take the one meant to fit Finn home and bury it in the farthest corner of the attic?

"Don't ask."

Carson found the one empty corner of his desk and leaned against it. "I drove Finn into Austin early this morning."

"How?"

"I was at Maggie's to pick up coffee before I drove in for an early meeting. He was there waiting for a cab."

The image of Finn walking down the highway away from her in the dark rose a lump in Amelia's throat. "How was he?"

"Miserable about sums it up."

Her constant heartache pitched into a searing pain that threatened a new bout of tears. She was so weary of feeling as if her heart had been trampled. Plum tired of trying to push the joy up from under all the hurt.

"He told me the whole story, Amelia. I don't think he planned to, or even wanted to, but he was so tired and hurt I think it sort of gushed out of him. Land sakes, but what that man has been through."

"It doesn't seem fair, does it?"

Carson ran a hand across his chin. "I tried, Amelia. I told him Little Horn would always welcome him. I gave him my cell number and offered to drive him back here after my meeting. I told him I thought you and he deserved a chance."

He didn't need more words to tell her his offer had been declined. "I'm sorry, Amelia."

She couldn't reply. She tried to be thankful that Carson had made the effort on her behalf, but her disappointment swallowed up any gratitude.

"He's doing it to protect you, if that makes any difference. He feels he's saving you from hurt by staying away."

"Saving me from hurt, is he?" The pain slipped out of her grasp, cutting a sharp, sour edge onto her words. "Well, it hasn't worked. I'm hurting now." She looked up at Carson. "He didn't even say goodbye."

"He knew you'd try to make him stay, and he didn't think he was strong enough to refuse."

Carson's eyes told her he knew his words were just making everything worse. She ought to thank him for trying, but the words stuck dry and false in her throat.

"I'm sorry, Amelia, I really am."

Amelia squeezed her eyes shut and pursed her lips tight. *You cannot go to pieces now. There are children out there who need you. Oh, Lord, how can I be joyful when my heart is broken in two...again?*

"You're one of the strongest people I know, Amelia. If anyone could have pulled Finn through this, it would have been you. He's just..."

Carson's words trailed off. How could any

words do justice to the sadness overtaking Finn? Who could judge anyone for buckling under the massive weight of what had happened to that man?

She could. She could because his descent into the pain had ripped her heart out and taken it down with him.

"Are you going to be all right?" Carson asked softly. She opened her eyes to see regret fill his features. "I'm sure Ruby and I can cover for you if you need to leave." He gestured at the mountain of gifts behind him. "You've done more than your share already."

Amelia forced her shoulders back and scraped in a breath. "I'm not leaving. This is the League Christmas party and this is what I do. Besides," she said, taking another deep breath even though it felt as if no air reached her lungs, "I don't think there's anyone else who can keep Byron's Santa from becoming a disaster."

"Byron? *Byron* is playing Santa this year?"

In another year, she might have found Carson's shock amusing. She nodded to the second suit. "Well, I had hoped to convince someone else to fill in, but..." She shook her head and flexed her fingers, determined to pull herself out of this.

"Amelia...do you need me to...?"

She held up her hand. "No. Don't. You've got a little nephew now. You can't possibly be Santa when he'd recognize you." She dabbed at her eyes. "Just tell me something happy. Tell me you are showering Ruby and Brandon with gifts. Tell me something happy. Anything."

Carson reluctantly complied. "We'll be announcing the wedding date on New Year's."

"Good. Wonderful. I'm happy for you, I really am. Now get back out there to your fiancée and your nephew. If you see Byron, tell him he'll need to be ready soon. I just… I just need a minute and then I'll be back out there to check on the food."

"Okay. I…" He left off, instead putting his hand on the door handle. "Well, okay."

Amelia was happy for Carson, she truly was. It was just that she ached in the spot under her ribs where her own happiness should have been. Where Finn still was, no matter how she tried to talk herself out of it. *I loved him. Oh, sweet Father, I love him still. What on earth am I supposed to do with that?* Gramps's words echoed in her head: *We don't always get to choose when and how folks become precious to us.*

It was as if Finn couldn't breathe in Austin. The lifeless quality of his apartment choked him from the moment he opened the door. Even though he remembered almost everything now, the familiar furnishings brought no comfort.

He'd held out past 3:00 p.m., forcing himself to

miss Carson's offer of a ride back to Little Horn. *You can't go back there*, he repeated over and over to himself as he bumbled around the dark apartment. As the sun went down and he hadn't even bothered to switch on a light. What was the point of light in this place? To him it could be dark even in the sunshine.

I can't do this. Finn groaned to God from where he'd slumped on the worn couch. *I can't go on living like this. It's not living. It's barely even existing. Why did You show me what it's like to live without this and then dump it all back onto me? It's so much worse now.*

Then go. The two words came to him out of the silence, like something snapping into place. He'd needed the pain to mean something, needed what had happened in Little Horn to make sense rather than feel like another cruel punishment. And the only thing that made sense, the only thing that held true if God was who Luther and so many people said He was, was Amelia. He'd been lost to be found. He'd lost his memory to break the chains of his past.

He didn't have to stop being who he was for Amelia. He did, however, need the courage to be who he *could* be. Finn didn't have that courage on his own—Amelia gave it to him. Amelia, who had more courage than anyone he'd ever known.

Then go. Finn fished through his kitchen

drawer to find the keys to his car. He'd rented a Jeep for the month of December and had been driving it that night he was going to the cabin— and he'd have to find out where that car was— but that detail wasn't important right now. What was important was he had a car. A car that could get him to Little Horn.

And right now, Little Horn was the only place on earth he wanted to be.

Chapter Twenty-One

The Christmas carol sing, usually one of Amelia's favorite parts of the annual League Christmas party, turned out to be heartbreaking. Every carol seemed connected to some moment or memory with Finn. She'd turned off the carol clock in the kitchen this afternoon, unable to stop the flood of memories that showed up with every hour chime. Mamie Stillwater and Eva Brooks had brought little baby Cody to the party, and the sight of that child dressed up in Christmas pajamas broke Amelia's heart as she thought of Finn's infant daughter, Annie.

Hearing sweet children's voices sing "Away in a Manger" was the worst of all. Amelia understood why Finn had rushed out of the food-truck courtyard during the final verse. "Bless all the dear children in thy tender care/ and fit us for heaven to live with thee there."

Finn was a good man. A loyal, honorable man who'd been through more than anyone she'd known. It seemed so unfair not only to pile that much tragedy into one life, but to make him the kind of man who felt he must endure it alone. Always quick to feel the nudge to help, the urge to help Finn rediscover even the smallest bit of joy in his life was a constant gnaw, an ache in Amelia's chest. Here she was, surrounded by happy, excited children, and she felt dark and sad. How much darker and sadder must Finn be in his self-imposed exile in Austin? She recalled the way he'd described his rooms. The hollowness of his life there. She kept hearing his voice say *I don't think I was a very happy man.*

You could be, Finn. God is big enough. I'm willing to risk it. You could be.

"O Little Town of Bethlehem" started, and Amelia tried to sing along, but her throat felt too dry and tight to let the words come out.

"Well, it seems I've found the party!" A voice came from the hallway, and the entire room turned to stare at a young woman who stood in the banquet room doorway.

Byron scowled at the party-crasher. "This is a private function. May I help you?"

Amelia found the young woman's face to be vaguely familiar, but she couldn't place it. The mystery guest tilted her chin up at Byron in defiance, parking one hand on her hip. "Depends if you know where baby Cody Stillwater is. I was told he and Miss Mamie were here."

The crowd murmured at her sharp tone. "And who are you to be looking for that baby?" Eva asked slowly. Tyler Granger put his hand protectively on his financée's shoulder as Eva clutched the child more tightly.

"I'm Vanessa Vane, that's who," the woman declared loudly as she walked toward Eva. "And I'm that baby's mama."

The room fell into startled silence. The adults darted looks back and forth between Vanessa and each other, while the children fidgeted at the interruption of their fun.

"Vanessa?" Byron's face was turning red as he angled himself between Vanessa and Eva—he didn't like anything marring the perfection of the League Christmas party, much less a scandalous shock like the one Vanessa had just delivered.

Mamie Stillwater worked her way around Eva and Tyler to face Vanessa. "It was you? You left my grandson on our doorstep?" The old woman's tone was so sharp Amelia couldn't decide if it was a question or an accusation.

Lucy, who'd been standing next to Amelia, leaned in. "And here I thought things couldn't get any more complicated around here." Even though Cody appeared on the Stillwater doorstep weeks ago and had been tested to prove he was a Stillwater, no one knew which of the Stillwater twins was his father and no one had any idea—until now—who the mother was. It had been just one more astounding event in Little Horn's recent history.

Amelia slanted a glance at her friend. "I was praying for a distraction, but this goes a bit far."

"I know I shouldn't have just left him with Grady like that, but things were...well, I don't care to go into all that here." Vanessa stepped closer to the child. "Hi there, little fella. Mommy missed you."

Mamie put her hand protectively over the child. "You didn't leave him with Grady. Grady is overseas on a mission. Strikes me as mighty odd that you don't know that—if you and Grady were as close as you claim."

"We were very close," Vera countered, holding her hands out to take the child from Eva. "Just ask Ben."

Everyone in the room responded to the bomb of that question. "We can't," Carson Thorn said sharply. "Ben is in the hospital in a coma."

"I had no idea." Vanessa at least looked genuinely distressed to learn the circumstances of the Stillwater men. "I'm so sorry."

"How could you leave this child on our doorstep without any explanation other than 'your turn'?" Mamie pulled herself up like the feisty grande dame that she was. "That's not how a decent mother behaves."

Vanessa squared her shoulders, as well. "I know everything ain't as it ought to be, but I'm ready to change that. I want a chance for us to be a real family."

"Miss Mamie, I wouldn't take her word for anything," Byron declared. "If you ask me, all she wants is…"

"Vanessa," Amelia cut in, hoping to avoid such a scene at a Christmas party in front of dozens of children, "you've been gone for ages. How did you know to find us here?"

"They told me at the ranch everyone was at a Christmas party. 'Course I knew it'd be here. I asked that guy standing out front anyway, just to be sure. He said he drove all the way from Austin. Why isn't he in here anyhow? Y'all get even more picky about who you let in to these things?"

Amelia looked over Vanessa's head to catch Carson's eye. She shouldn't allow herself to hope, but her heart leapt anyway. Carson shrugged as if to say *Could be.* Willing herself to breathe, Amelia smiled politely at Vanessa and said, "Will y'all excuse me for a minute?" She forced her feet to walk out into the hallway, then lost the battle with her optimism and ran for the door.

She yanked it open and scanned the League

office front yard. There, at the edge of the lights leaning up against the sign, stood Finn.

Finn had been so sure this was the right thing to do. The whole drive out to Little Horn, his conviction strengthened until he was sure he would bolt out of the car, swoop into that party and claim Amelia for his own.

Now that he was here, he lost his nerve. After all, he was still a Ranger and had to return to duty eventually. The risks that had taken Belinda and Annie's life were still part of his job. Two hours ago he'd been sure choosing to make a go of it with Amelia was the right thing to do. Now, standing outside this building knowing her life and friends and warmth were all inside, it felt selfish. What could he possibly give her in return for all she'd give him? All she had already given him?

He'd almost walked in with that young woman who'd stopped to ask if this was the League Christmas party. No—he couldn't saunter in there like any other guest. His walking through that door would mean everything. He had to do it on his own, with intention, not in the shadow of someone else.

Maybe tomorrow. Maybe after I make it through Christmas. It's bound to be awful, and

*she loves all that stuff too much for me to dampen
it for her.*

He was leaning against the headquarters sign,
trying to force his feet to turn back toward the
car, when the door flung open. She was in shadows, lit from behind as she was in the doorway,
but there was no mistaking Amelia's silhouette.

Finn had retreated to the darkness, staying just
outside the circle of light thrown by the landscap-
ing floodlights that surrounded the building. Still,
he could see—clearly, in a way that struck him
like a jolt to his chest—the moment she caught
sight of him. There was a second where she just
stood there, grinding Finn's pulse to a halt. He
held his breath and told himself that he had no
right to thrust his broken life into her world, that
it was better for everyone if she turned around
and shut the door.

Then she nearly leaped off the front step,
practically stumbling in her high heels to take
the sidewalk at a run. The grass between them
tripped her up even further, and he started toward
her to catch her if she fell. Determined to save
her the way she'd saved him.

Amelia tumbled into him, throwing her arms
around his neck. The joy of it, the all-out welcome of it split his heart wide open. Not loving
this woman was simply impossible. There was
Amelia, and there was the rest of the dull world

without her. At this moment, he wanted the world with Amelia more than anything and Finn knew he would risk, do or sacrifice anything to stay beside her.

He wrapped his arms around her, leaning his head into the mass of blond curls. He'd spent the past hours dreaming of touching those curls, needing to hold this woman in his arms. Until now, their touch had been careful and restrained. Now he held her with all his might, nearly laughing at the gleefully fierce way she held him. How could he have ever thought walking away from this woman was the right thing to do?

She pulled back to look at him, eyes gleaming, no hint of reservation anywhere in their blue depths. "You came back."

There were a dozen replies to that, but Finn chose the only one that counted. He leaned down and kissed her. He'd intended it to be gentle, but it didn't stay that way for long. After all, Amelia Klondike never did anything halfway—she kissed him back but good. The dreary hollowness that had been his constant companion vanished, replaced by the glow of…it took him a second to name the feeling, strange as it was…hope.

"I couldn't stay away," he said, brushing one hand against her cheek, delighted at the sparkle it brought to her eyes. "I don't know how we're going to do this but…"

"But we'll do it." She cut him off, shaking her head and tightening her grip. "We'll make it work."

"I want to," Finn agreed, leaning his forehead down to touch hers. The loneliness fell off him like a broken shell, and he felt new and alive. "I didn't think I could ever…" He didn't even want to finish the sentence, much preferring to kiss her than hunt for words that didn't seem to matter anymore.

There was a ruckus behind them, and Finn broke away to see Luther standing in the doorway.

"What the… Oh," the old man said, pretending at annoyance but breaking into a wide smile when he caught sight of Finn. "Well, now, ain't that something to put under the tree."

Finn heard Carson's voice from the hallway behind. "Luther, what's going on out there?"

Luther chuckled. "Nothing to see here, boys. Head on back to your party." With a huge thumbs-up gesture, Luther waved his cane at whomever was trying to peer around him and headed back into the building.

Finn found himself laughing. When was the last time he'd laughed? "I'm glad to know Luther approves."

"Well, Gramps has always said Bug is an excellent judge of character. That dog adores you."

She looked up at him, eyes wide and wondrous. "He's not alone."

"I love you, Amelia. Do you think that's enough?"

"It's the start of everything, Finn. I love you, too. And yes, I think it will be enough. I want a life with you, and if you're willing to work at it as hard as I am, how can it not be enough?"

It was she who kissed him then, as if sealing the promise. Finn clung to her, feeling how her light seeped into all the dark corners of his life he thought lost for good. "I can't believe I'm saying this, but I'm glad for what happened. I'm glad I lost my memory so that you could find me."

She ran one hand through his hair, the sensation crackling through him like sparks on a dark night. "God does seem to have a flair for the dramatic, doesn't He?"

"You could say that."

She fingered the stray hairs falling over his forehead. "Come inside and celebrate Christmas." Her words told him she knew the weight of that invitation for him.

"I want to," he said, surprised at how much he did. "I'm not exactly dressed for a party." In fact, he was a mess. In his rush to get to Little Horn he'd not shaved or changed since yesterday, and he imagined he looked more like a rumpled hobo than a party guest.

"Well, about that…" Amelia got a strange look in her eyes. "I happen to have a suit inside that's just your size."

That stumped him. "What do you mean?"

"Come inside. Finn Brannigan, you're about to dive into Christmas headfirst." She pulled on his arm, and he felt himself surrender—gladly—to Amelia's wave of holiday mayhem.

Just before they reached the door, Amelia turned and planted one last kiss on his lips. "How are you at 'Ho, ho, ho'?"

Finn blinked at her. "Horrible."

She winked. "I can work with that."

Chapter Twenty-Two

Amelia swept up more wrapping paper while Lucy and her friend Chloe Miner held open the garbage bag. "Thanks for pitching in to help clean up, Chloe," Amelia offered. "We certainly can't fault Eva for needing to get Miss Mamie and baby Cody home early to sort things out with Vanessa."

"Your stepsister sure surprised everyone tonight," Lucy said, tying off one garbage bag and reaching for another. The banquet room was practically knee-deep in discarded gift wrap—Amelia really had outdone herself in the gifts this year. "Did you know she was coming back? Did you even know she'd had a baby?"

"*Ex*-stepsister. My dad wasn't married to her mom for very long. And believe me," Chloe replied, "I was as shocked as the rest of you."

Lucy looked at Finn, who was helping Carson put away chairs at the far side of the room. Finn still had the Santa suit on, with the jacket hanging open, the hat falling lazily to one side and the fake white beard spilling out of one pocket. "Well, at least some of tonight's surprises were pleasant ones." Lucy elbowed Amelia. "And not just because it saved us all from Santa Byron."

Chloe laughed. "Really. Whatever made you think *that* would work?"

Amelia narrowed her eyes playfully. "I was fresh out of volunteers."

"Well, there'll be no shortage of Christmas cheer at your house this season," Lucy teased. "I'm happy for you. Y'all can make it work, I know it. I've never seen two people more taken with each other. Even when Finn had that ridiculous beard on, you were staring at him with your mouth hanging open."

Amelia swatted Lucy with a wad of candy-cane wrapping paper. "I was not." Even as she spoke, Amelia felt her eyes wander toward the handsome guy in the silly red suit.

"Yeah," said Chloe as she poked Amelia's arm, "you were. You still are. It's kind of cute, in a sugarcoated, gooey sort of way."

"Hey, if anyone's earned a happy ending, it's you." Lucy sighed as she tamped down the piles of paper. "Now just gift-wrap a certain cattle rustler for me, and we can call the year a success."

"I thought you had a lead suspect," Amelia

asked as she pulled a red bow down off one of the wall sconces.

"I did," Lucy replied, "until he alibied out this afternoon. And while Boone is not going to win any citizen-of-the year awards, we both know he's not our guy, either. I hate to say it, but we're back to square one with no firm leads."

"Did you ask Santa to bring you a closed case for Christmas?" Finn's voice came from behind Amelia, rich and warm. Everything about him had transformed tonight—his eyes, the set of his shoulders, even the tone of his voice. All the obstacles were still in front of them, but they seemed infinitely smaller now. Based on tonight, the New Year was going to be a wonderful one.

Lucy clasped her hands together. "Please, Santa, may I have a perpetrator behind bars for Christmas?"

"Are you on my Nice list?" A joke, from Finn? He really had come back to life tonight.

Lucy smirked. "I think there's only one lady on your Nice list, Santa Finn."

Amelia felt Finn's arm slip around her waist. "The sheriff knows her facts."

"You know," Chloe said knowingly, "I'm pretty sure Lucy and I can finish up here. Seems to me Santa and his pretty little helper have earned the rest of the night off."

Amelia looked at Lucy. As chair of the League

Christmas party, she'd always felt it her job to be the last to leave. She was doing her best to stay on task, but right now all she wanted to do was go home and stay up all night talking to Finn. She had a week's worth of things to say to him.

Lucy waved her off. "Oh, go. Y'all are getting hard to watch as it is. What did you call it, Chloe?"

"Sugarcoated ooey-gooey."

Amelia could only laugh. She did feel sugarcoated and ooey-gooey. In every best sense of the word.

"Come on," Finn said with a dashing grin. "I've got a sleigh outside and everything."

"I've got an old man and a fat dog who will be thrilled to know you're staying in Little Horn." She turned to her friends, warmed by their encouraging smiles. "Merry Christmas to all," Amelia called as she let Finn lead her from the room. *And to all a good night*, she thought, her heart full of grace and thanks. *God bless us, everyone*.

* * * * *

Dear Reader,

Romance author is probably the only career where having amnesia is a professional asset! Having experienced a bout of Temporary Global Amnesia myself in 2010, I was instantly drawn to Finn's story. I lost only my short-term memory and some circumstantial facts for four days, but it was enough to recall the fear and frustration Finn must have endured. Lest you worry, I fully recovered; I remember everything except the onset of my episode. It gave me a unique and hearty respect for our brain—it truly is the human organ we least understand.

The heart, however, can make all things new. Amelia's heart learns how to truly heal as she helps Finn recover. And who can underestimate the recuperative powers of a lovable dog!

If you enjoyed this story, please let me know. You can find me on Facebook, Twitter, at www. alliepleiter.com and via email at allie@alliepleter. com.

Allie

LARGER-PRINT BOOKS!

GET 2 FREE LARGER-PRINT NOVELS PLUS 2 FREE MYSTERY GIFTS

Love Inspired®

SUSPENSE
RIVETING INSPIRATIONAL ROMANCE

Larger-print novels are now available...

REQUEST YOUR FREE BOOKS!
2 FREE WHOLESOME ROMANCE NOVELS
IN LARGER PRINT
PLUS 2
FREE
MYSTERY GIFTS

✤✤✤✤✤✤✤✤✤✤✤✤✤✤✤✤✤✤✤✤✤✤✤✤

HEARTWARMING™

✤✤✤✤✤✤✤✤✤✤✤✤✤✤✤✤✤✤✤✤✤✤✤✤

Wholesome, tender romances

YES! Please send me 2 FREE Harlequin® Heartwarming Larger-Print novels and my 2 FREE mystery gifts (gifts worth about $10). After receiving them, if I don't wish to receive any more books, I can return the shipping statement marked "cancel." If I don't cancel, I will receive 4 brand-new larger-print novels every month and be billed just $5.24 per book in the U.S. or $5.99 per book in Canada. That's a savings of at least 19% off the cover price. It's quite a bargain! Shipping and handling is just 50¢ per book in the U.S. and 75¢ per book in Canada.* I understand that accepting the 2 free books and gifts places me under no obligation to buy anything. I can always return a shipment and cancel at any time. Even if I never buy another book, the two free books and gifts are mine to keep forever.

161/361 IDN GHX2

Name	(PLEASE PRINT)

Address	Apt. #

City	State/Prov.	Zip/Postal Code

Signature (if under 18, a parent or guardian must sign)

Mail to the **Reader Service**:
IN U.S.A.: P.O. Box 1867, Buffalo, NY 14240-1867
IN CANADA: P.O. Box 609, Fort Erie, Ontario L2A 5X3

* Terms and prices subject to change without notice. Prices do not include applicable taxes. Sales tax applicable in N.Y. Canadian residents will be charged applicable taxes. Offer not valid in Quebec. This offer is limited to one order per household. Not valid for current subscribers to Harlequin Heartwarming larger-print books. All orders subject to credit approval. Credit or debit balances in a customer's account(s) may be offset by any other outstanding balance owed by or to the customer. Please allow 4 to 6 weeks for delivery. Offer available while quantities last.

Your Privacy—The Reader Service is committed to protecting your privacy. Our Privacy Policy is available online at www.ReaderService.com or upon request from the Reader Service.

We make a portion of our mailing list available to reputable third parties that offer products we believe may interest you. If you prefer that we not exchange your name with third parties, or if you wish to clarify or modify your communication preferences, please visit us at www.ReaderService.com/consumerschoice or write to us at Reader Service Preference Service, P.O. Box 9062, Buffalo, NY 14240-9062. Include your complete name and address.

HWI5

YES! Please send me **The Montana Mavericks Collection** in Larger Print. This collection begins with 3 FREE books and 2 FREE gifts (gifts valued at approx. $20.00 retail) in the first shipment, along with the other first 4 books from the collection! If I do not cancel, I will receive 8 monthly shipments until I have the entire 51-book Montana Mavericks collection. I will receive 2 or 3 FREE books in each shipment and I will pay just $4.99 US/ $5.89 CDN for each of the other four books in each shipment, plus $2.99 for shipping and handling per shipment.*If I decide to keep the entire collection, I'll have paid for only 32 books, because 19 books are FREE! I understand that accepting the 3 free books and gifts places me under no obligation to buy anything. I can always return a shipment and cancel at any time. My free books and gifts are mine to keep no matter what I decide.

263 HCN 2404   463 HCN 2404

Name	(PLEASE PRINT)	
Address		Apt. #
City	State/Prov.	Zip/Postal Code

Signature (if under 18, a parent or guardian must sign)

Mail to the **Reader Service**:

IN U.S.A.: P.O. Box 1867, Buffalo, NY 14240-1867
IN CANADA: P.O. Box 609, Fort Erie, Ontario L2A 5X3

MMLPBPA15